GRIZZLY TALES

'CAUTIONARY TALES FOR LOVERS OF SQUEAM'

JAMIE RIX

illustrated by Steven Pattison

JUST CLOSE THE BOOK.
PUT IT BACK ON THE SHELF.
AND RUN!

Orion
Children's Books

For Louisa and Richard

First published in Great Britain in 2007
by Orion Children's Books
a division of the Orion Publishing Group Ltd
Orion House
5 Upper St Martin's Lane
London WC2H 9EA

A catalogue record for this book is available from the British Library.

Printed in Great Britain

ISBN 978 1 84255 550 7

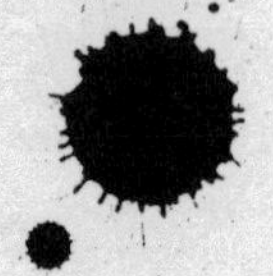

SAFETY
CARD

SAFETY CARD

for The Twin-Engined Grizzly Paperback

In case of an emergency (such as an urgent need to wet yourself in fear or discovering a split in one of your sides) you will find a Life Jacket on page 50 and a pair of safety goggles also on page 50. Cut them out and put them on.

No sharp objects may be taken into this book in case the bad children inside get hold of them. Please surrender all sharp objects at the door. Sharp objects include knives, compasses, combs and scissors.*

Please adopt the safety position if you find yourself too scared to read on.

Enjoy your read and we look forward to welcoming you aboard another Grizzly Paperback soon!

*(Sorry. We forgot. You won't be able to cut out the Life Jacket and safety goggles after all. Oh well, it's wet trousers and spilled guts on the floor for you!)

Welcome to

The Hothell Darkness

Breakfast 7.30am – 9.30am.

No parents unless by prior arrangement with the management. It is our job to make you feel at home. If there is anything we can do to make your stay with us more uncomfortable please do not hesitate to ring the front desk. It is manned day and night by a stupid girl who snapped off her arms when she stood up and waved out of a car's sunroof while it was speeding through a tunnel; so don't be surprised if she doesn't pick up.

Hello. I didn't expect to see you back so soon.

Don't go. Your room is now ready.

You didn't know you were staying?

No. None of our guests does, but you are. You're a child and The Darkness is a place where children stay for ever. In you heart, you know that you belong here.

Let's see how bad you really are.

ANSWER TRUTHFULLY!

1) Have you ever shouted loudly near an old person? *Tut tut.*

2) Do you sometimes wish that your parents would put their heads in a food blender and leave you alone? *Haven't we all.*

3) Do you eat with your mouth full? *You big pig!*

4) If you could bury the worst experiences of your life in a box to get rid of them, would your teachers be the first thing you put in? *That's right, nobody likes a teacher. Crabby know-alls!*

5) Are you smaller today than you will be tomorrow?

If you have answered YES to all of these questions you are BAD enough to stay. If you have answered NO to any of the above you have lied through your teeth so you are staying too!

You may help pass eternity by reading our visitor's book or, as I prefer to call it, The Book of Grizzly Tales. Measure your own badness against the stories of our wicked guests. These stories tell of children who have all fallen foul of grown-ups. You know grown-ups: those big, shouty, snoring, law-making machines that make your life so unbearable. Shall I tell you a secret?

Don't eat me again! Please don't eat me again!

Dig-diggerdy-do!

Bubble, bubble, bubble

Boo hoo hoo! Boo hoo hoo!

WHAT DID YOU SAY? SPEAK UP! I CAN'T HEAR YOU.

Aaaaaaaaaaaaagh! This is a nightmare!

Ignore them. Come closer. Don't be scared.

Really close. I'm not going to grab you or nibble your ear.

As close as you dare. Put your eyeball on the page.

They all work for me!

It's true! How do you think I know when you're being bad? I don't have all-seeing eyes. I rely on my grown up spies!

Some grown-ups FIND naughty children and despatch them down here, dead or alive! Others turn GOOD children BAD. But most are under instructions to TEACH bad children a LESSON they will never, ever, ever forget!

How scary is that? It means you'll NEVER be able to trust a grown-up again! Not at home, not in the street and certainly not at school!

These days there's a lot of old tripe talked about school dinners, about how school food was SO MUCH BETTER for children in the olden days when they drenched their bread in dripping and dipped their chips in licker and horse fat. How much healthier it was, say the experts, when children ate brains for elevenses and lungs and lights for lunch; when children ate heart, kidneys,

liver, intestines and testicles, and went back for more. They say that today's children – that's YOU – are too sensitive to eat internal organs. That you grimace at guts and freak out at offal, which is why you eat nothing but chicken nuggets!

But I say, LET THEM EAT CHICKEN NUGGETS, because I know what goes into the making of them. One thing's for sure, it's NOT chicken!

WANTED
GROWN-UPS
who can bring up BAD CHILDREN

If you are a GROWN-UP who likes being particularly unpleasant and can dish out punishments without turning a hair, this is the job for you.

Do something useful with your life.

Join the Hothell Darkness Recruitment Police!

SPY on your own children!

SHOP the offspring of friends and neighbours!

CLEAR the streets of bad children and earn money while having fun!

FANTASTIC REWARDS

A world without children . . . for a start!

DON'T DELAY, BETRAY THEM TODAY!

Please display this poster in both the sitting room window and the downstairs loo so that all passing grown ups can see it.

JAMIE'S SCHOOL DINNERS

Jamie loved chicken nuggets. He loved all junk food, but chicken nuggets came top. He always said that if he was abducted by aliens and told that he could only eat one type of food for the rest of his life, he would choose chicken nuggets.

Other people, especially Mrs Saladbowl, the mother of Jamie's best friend Tom, thought Jamie was crazy. 'You want MORE chicken nuggets!' she gasped when Jamie went round for tea. 'Are you mad?'

'I love chicken nuggets,' dribbled Jamie.

'As a matter of fact, he *is* mad,' said Tom. 'It's the lack of nutrition in his diet, it's shrunk his brain.'

In fact, Jamie's brain hadn't shrunk, because it had never been big in the first place. Up until the age of three he hadn't had a brain at all, then his parents had given him theirs and

now it was the size of two peanuts. They had made a ceremony out of it on a wet Sunday afternoon, going down on their knees and offering up their brains on a plush purple cushion.

'We want you to have these,' Jamie's father had said. 'We don't need them any more.'

'You can put our two little brains together,' his mother had whispered, 'to make one big brain.'

'I don't know what to say,' Jamie had said.

'Well, pop them in,' she had said, 'and maybe you'll think of something.'

Jamie's parents had stopped using their brains on the day they had explained to Jamie that a cola and a cheeseburger was a perfectly balanced meal.

'What do you mean by balanced?' he had asked.

'Well,' Jamie's mother had said, placing a cheeseburger in one hand and a can of cola in the other, then raising her arms until they were level with her shoulders. 'You can hold one in each hand, see. And because they're about the same weight it's balanced.'

'She couldn't fall over even if she wanted to,' Jamie's father had said. By now, Jamie's mother had eaten the

cheeseburger and replaced it with a pound of lard.

'Actually, a pound of lard would balance too,' she had added.

'It would,' Jamie's father had said.

'Unless I went and ate it,' Jamie's mother had said, tearing off the paper with her teeth and licking the lard like ice cream, 'because I would, because I love lard!'

***

Even before they had given their brains away, Jamie's parents weren't the sharpest knives in the block. And now that Jamie had their brains he thought exactly as they did. It was hardly surprising, therefore, that he thought processed slops were delicious. He loved the taste, and because he wouldn't eat anything he hadn't tasted before, all he ever ate was junk.

And if it's true that you are what you eat that meant that Jamie was JUNK too, which is why, quite frankly, nobody cried when he disappeared. Because he DID disappear, under villainous circumstances!

By the time Jamie went to big school, he was a

huge, indolent lump. Eleven years of fatty foods had changed his shape. He was as round as a beach ball with skin so tight that he looked like an overstuffed sausage. His friends from primary school didn't want to hang out with him any more.

'Why?' said Jamie, stuffing his face with a cheesy chilli kebab.

'Because all you ever think about is food,' said Tom Saladbowl.

'And if any of us have sweets in our pockets,' added Bethany Bramley, 'you steal them off us and stuff them in your face without even asking.'

'I love sweets,' grinned Jamie.

'And if I'm sitting next to you on a bus,' chipped in Mini Milo, whose doctors were predicting a growth spurt any day now, 'you sit on me without even knowing I'm there. It's horrible!'

'Take the train!' slobbered Jamie, who didn't seem to care that he was losing his friends just so long as he never lost his taste for bad food.

* * *

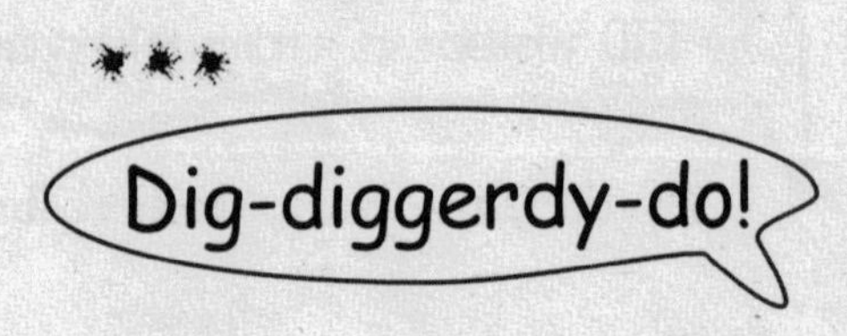

Jamie's fatness worried his new headmistress – a pernickety woman who hand-fed any pupil who wasn't eating five portions of fresh fruit and vegetables a day. She was a firm believer that healthy food built healthy pupils and healthy pupils did better in the league tables. But of course she hadn't bargained on Jamie's stubbornness. The first time she tried to push a carrot between his lips he nearly bit her fingers off.

'I won't eat it,' he said. 'It's dirty!' The second time, she was more careful. She grated the carrot, held his nose and sprinkled it down his throat, but Jamie sicked it all up again and wiped his lips on her skirt.

The third time, she tried an altogether different approach. She burst into tears. 'Oh please,' she blubbed, sliding a chicken salad across the table to tempt him. 'Won't you at least *try* something?'

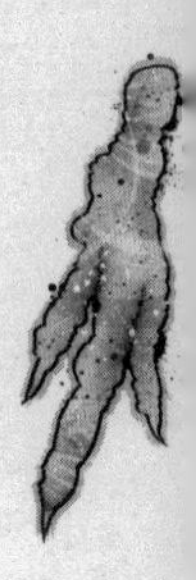

'You want me to try something?' said Jamie, defiantly.

'Oh would you,' she sobbed theatrically. 'For little old me.'

'All right, I'll try this—' he said, opening his

lungs and screaming at the top of his voice, 'YUCK! IT'S DISGUSTING!' Then he hurled the chicken salad against the wall and lowered his voice to a snarl. 'Now do you believe I don't like it?' he said.

Jamie had made his point. The headmistress was not going to win. But even if he wouldn't eat healthy food, she still had a responsibility to see that Jamie didn't starve. Accordingly, she phoned up a dinner lady who advertised herself in the local paper thus:

SCHOOL DINNER LADY FOR HIRE

I can't chop. I can't peel.
I can't cook.
Call Ambrosine to solve all your catering problems.

Well, Jamie was a problem so it made sense to call her. The headmistress was worried, however, by one tiny thing. 'What do you mean, you can't cook?' she said.

'Fresh food,' said Ambrosine on the other end of

the telephone. 'I can't cook fresh food, but I'm a whiz with chicken nuggets and a microwave.'

'You mean you can reheat junk?'

Ambrosine cackled with a laugh that sounded like a knife rattling in a ribcage. 'Yes, dear,' she wheezed, 'that's my skill. Reheating junk! It's so much less effort!'

And Jamie was JUNK, remember? You don't think, by any chance, that Ambrosine cooking Jamie's School Dinners might be a recipe for disaster, do you?

* * *

The next day, during first break, an air horn cut through the chatter of voices in the playground and sent the children scurrying for safety. Seconds later, a huge silver tanker full to the brim with Fatty Fry's Cooking Oil pulled through the school gates and screeched to a halt on the five-a-side football pitch. The door to the cab flew open and a pair of black leather ankle boots jumped down on to the concrete. It wasn't the unnaturally curly toes or the long, icy black shadow that scared away the children, but the face. It was shaped like a crescent moon with a prominent chin and forehead, rotten teeth and a hooked nose which had a single black hair protruding from the tip. It was the new dinner lady.

'You must be Jamie,' she hissed at the only child left in the playground.

'How did you know?' he replied.

'I can smell you,' she sniffed. 'Overweight children give off a powerful stench when they're ripe for the picking.' She took a small jar of white powder out of her pocket, unscrewed the lid, dipped in a teaspoon and licked off the sugar with a look of such eye-bulging rapture that she temporarily lost her footing.

'Careful,' said Jamie, steadying her with his hand. 'Are you the woman who's come to cook my dinners?'

'Don't touch me!' she snapped.

Jamie was unnerved by the coldness of her voice and took a step backwards. 'But don't you want to know what I like to eat?'

'It's obvious,' she spat. 'Now take me to your larder! We must feed you up immediately!' Which is exactly what she did.

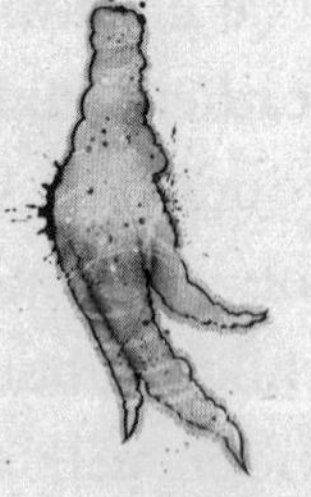

***

Over the next few weeks, Jamie grew fatter with every processed school dinner she shoved down his throat. Within a month her nickname for him was being chanted in the playground.

'Little goose! Little goose!

Too fat for chocolate mousse!'

But Jamie wasn't bothered by these taunts so long as the junk food kept coming. And come it did, by the bucketful! Each day brought a new surprise.

'These are bacon drummers,' said Ambrosine, handing a plate of what looked like chicken drumsticks through the serving hatch.

'Are these going to taste of bacon?' asked Jamie as he greedily snatched his lunch.

'They might do,' she said, 'but there again they might taste of fish.'

'So what are they?'

'Once they were legs,' she replied mysteriously.

'From a pig?'

'Unlikely,' she said, as he took a bite. 'Is it tickling your tastebuds?'

'It's delicious,' said Jamie. 'Tastes like old books. You know – paper and cardboard with a hint of ink.'

'More?' she twinkled.

'MORE!' he yelled greedily. This soon became the pattern for lunch. Not just firsts and seconds, but thirds and fourths as well, and Ambrosine only allowed him to leave the table when he was in actual pain from T.T.T. – Tummy Touching Table!

***

Instead of turkey at Christmas she made him chicken nuggets shaped like feet. 'My signature dish!' she explained.

'What does that mean?' asked Jamie.

'This is the dish they all die for!' she squealed. 'Now go and sit down, my little goose. Today, in honour of my culinary genius, I shall serve you at table.' A few moments later, she emerged from the kitchen carrying a domed silver platter. Then, bowing low like a toadying waiter, she removed the lid and presented the feet for Jamie to sniff. 'Made from the rankest cuts that I wouldn't even feed to a dog,' she boasted, 'I have extracted all the taste and goodness, then pumped it full of artificial flavourings and preservatives to give this dish a shelf life longer than radioactive uranium.'

Jamie's eyes lit up. 'Is it chicken?' he asked.

'No,' she replied, 'but it would be chicken not to eat it. Enjoy!'

And a jolly stuffed Christmas he had too!

***

As New Year turned into spring, Jamie gorged on fat, salt, grease, sugar and enough chemicals to raise the dead. It didn't matter what Ambrosine put in his food, Jamie ate everything, so long as it wasn't fresh. So when he found a radio receiver poking out of his chocolate pizza like a miniature Eiffel Tower, he didn't bat an eyelid. Down it went with everything else, battery pack and all.

But the junk food was taking its toll. After six months of solid eating Jamie was not only fat, with six chins and legs as wide as his waist, but now he was spotty as well. His face had erupted in a plague of yellow-headed zits and around his neck where the skin hung in folds like curtain swags, mushrooms had started to grow. The chemicals in Ambrosine's meals had mushed his brain so that he couldn't concentrate for more than five seconds at a time. He was lazy and forgetful, so much so that

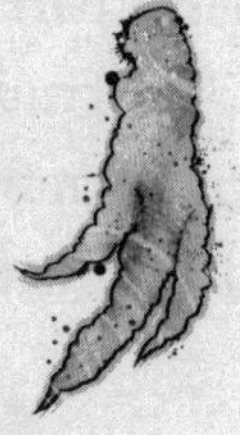

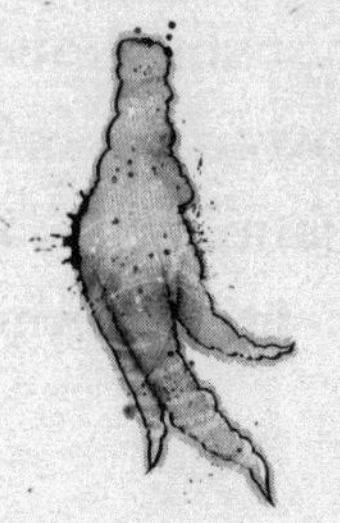

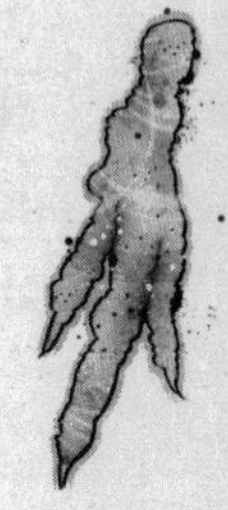

his parents never knew if he was coming home or not. On more than one occasion, Jamie found himself wandering the streets of a strange town trying to remember where he lived.

Mind you, Jamie's parents were just as bad as their son. They were both the size of barrels and because they ate the same junk food as Jamie every night, *their* memories were shot to pieces as well. Not only that, but their get up and go had long since got up and gone. It would be no exaggeration to say that the greatest misfortune in Jamie's life was having them as parents.

True, but none of us can choose our parents, can we? More's the pity!

***

On one particular Tuesday morning, the listlessness in Jamie's house was as bad as it had ever been. Neither Jamie nor his parents had remembered their own names for a week. Jamie went off to school leaving his parents getting ready for work. When he returned home later that afternoon, he found them sitting in the hall with their coats still on.

'Hello!' said Jamie, walking through the front door. 'I'm . . .' There was a long pause while Jamie tried to remember what he was going to say. Eventually his father filled the gap.

'Home?' he said.

'No. Jamie,' said Jamie. 'I'm Jamie. I've remembered! Have you had a nice day?'

'We were going out this morning,' said his father, 'but we forgot where we were going, so we've just sat here instead.'

'Quite nice,' said Jamie's mother.

'I'm exhausted,' yawned Jamie, slumping to the floor for a kip.

This was her moment! Ambrosine's eyelids flickered as she half woke up. Then, brushing the cockroaches off her pillow, she dragged her twisted body out of bed and slapped in her teeth and eye.

***

Jamie was too tired to eat supper. While his parents sat up and watched a damp patch on the wall, thinking it was the television, he went to bed early.

'Phewwwww!' he sighed. 'All that remembering my own name has worn me out! Oh, I can see why,' he said, as

he caught sight of his alarm clock, 'it's past my bedtime!' It was five o'clock in the afternoon.

One hour later, as sea-sick prawns splattered against the glass in the windows, a bell rang in a steel-ringed kitchen in the North Atlantic. From this she knew that Jamie was asleep. A crooked finger, dripping with pink gunge, switched on a radio-controlled transmitter.

***

Hundreds of miles away, deep inside Jamie's stomach, the radio receiver burst into life with a high-pitched beep. His legs swung out of bed and his feet placed themselves on the floor. Then he stood up and started sleepwalking: down the stairs, out of the house and on to the street. He didn't wake. Not even when the driver asked him for his ticket on the night bus; not even when he stumbled across a runway in front of a jumbo jet; not even when the ferry left without him and he fell off the jetty into the cold North Sea; not even when the sharks circled as he swam the long, dark miles to the island . . . Ambrosine's Island, where junk food kids were junked!

By the way, I just happen to have six million ferry tickets to Ambrosine's Island. If you're a fan of junk food, see me afterwards.

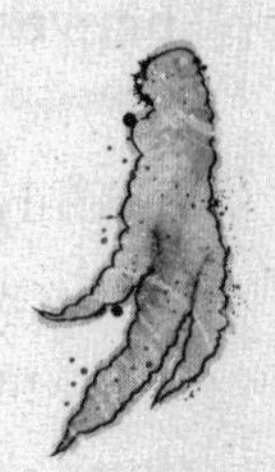

When Jamie woke up he was lying on a wooden chopping board in the kitchen of a stone-walled castle. He was not tied down, but his head felt groggy and he couldn't move.

'Ohhh . . . I feel like I've been hit over the head,' he groaned.

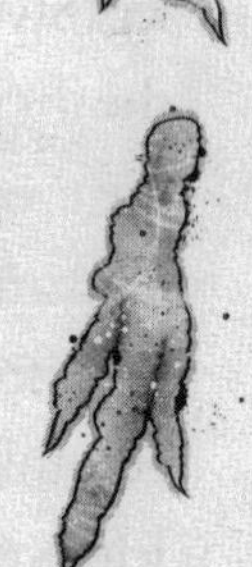

'That'll be the monosodium glutamate,' said a familiar voice. 'It can leave some children with a bit of a hangover.'

It was a struggle to open his eyes, but when he did, Jamie saw Ambrosine standing directly behind him talking to someone on the other wall. He turned his head and saw a television camera.

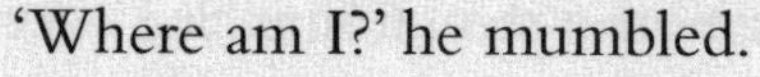

'Where am I?' he mumbled.

'On telly,' hissed Ambrosine fiercely. 'This is a cookery programme for the Witch and Warlock Channel. So quieten down.'

Bubble, bubble, bubble

And you can shut up as well!

Best programmes on the Witch and Warlock Channel are *Witch of the Day*, *Strictly Come Broomsticking*, *Celebrity Ready Steady Stake-Burning* and *Dr Which*. I never miss them!

Duly chastened, Jamie watched Ambrosine turn back to the camera and smile. 'Next, you want to add plenty of salt and sugar,' she said, throwing a bucket of each over Jamie. The grains went up his nose and made him cough. She grabbed the back of his head and tugged him into an upright position, so that his back was straight and his mouth was forced open like the beak of a gosling at feeding time. 'Then simply add your stuffing!' she declared. 'That's three pounds of unrendered fat, bone and gristle, half a pint of blood, some e-numbers and a handful of unwanted eyelashes.'

She picked up a stainless-steel funnel and a basin of pink gunk, put the funnel into Jamie's mouth and forced the stuffing down Jamie's throat with a spoon. 'My good little goose,' she whispered under her breath. 'Now you're going to find out what meat I use in my chicken nuggets.'

Then she raised her head and once again

addressed the camera. 'And keep that going in until he's full. Now, this particular child shouldn't need much stuffing, because he's nice and plump already. So, tamp it all down . . . There we go. Last bit . . .'

Unable to move, Jamie had no choice but to suffer in silence. And suffer he did, because with every prod of her wooden spoon the stuffing was driven deeper into his body. As more stuffing went in he swelled and swelled and his skin grew tighter and tighter until finally it could stand the strain no longer. There was a moment of pain-free bliss and then he burst!

'And there it is,' she cried, as the kitchen rained Jamie. 'The fat child explodes!' Ambrosine was delighted with herself and hurried on to the next stage of her recipe. 'All you have to do now is scrape him off the walls into a mixing bowl and mould this gorgeous squidge into any shape that takes your fancy,' she said, taking a handful of Jamie out of the bowl and moulding it into the shape of a foot. Then she dipped the foot in breadcrumbs and dropped it into a deep fat fryer. 'That should take about twenty minutes. You'll know it's ready when it's burnt and inedible. And there we

have it. What could be simpler? Perfect chicken nuggets, fit for the school dinner table, every time!'

***

Three days later, after the damp patch had dried out and Jamie's parents had nothing left to watch, they happened across their son's empty bed.

'Who sleeps here?' asked his empty-headed father.

'I don't know,' said his mother. They had completely forgotten that they'd ever had a son, which was lucky, because it saved them both from needless heartache. At 12.30 pm on that very same day, their son Jamie was served up on a plate to a gormless looking student in Scunthorpe, who ate half and scraped the rest into the slops bowl!

I went and had a look in that slops bowl but I couldn't tell which half got scraped in. All of Jamie is pink gunge now so there are no distinguishing features like arms or ears. And you. . . can't get a conversation out of him so you can't tell which end's got the mouth in. Still. I brought him back here and he lives in The Darkness now. I had a bit of grouting needed doing so I've put him in the shower room . . . in between the tiles!

And just in case you're wondering: YES. It's a very big wall and there's LOADS MORE grouting to do! So EAT UP, JUNKERS!

Throughout this book I shall be giving you helpful hints on how to deal with gruesome grown-ups. I shall entitle this advice Helpful Hints on How To Deal With Gruesome Grown-Ups.

Helpful Hints on How To Deal With Gruesome Grown-ups

1. RESPECT YOUR ELDERS

When a new dinner lady appears at your school and offers you chicken nugget feet and bacon drummers, you know what to do. Remember your manners: be polite to your elders and betters and accept the plate with a slight bowing of the head, a lowering of the eyes and a firm, but unchallenging 'Thank you'. Then eat it all up! And when you explode I'll see you down here for a shower. Looking forward to it. Splish splash!

Schools would be the best places for me to find bad children, were it not for the fact that teachers make the worst spies.

'Oh we can't spy on the children,' they whine. 'It would be a violation of the trust between teacher and pupil!' They CLAIM they don't know how to use a thumbscrew or administer a Vulcan death grip and they strongly disapprove of iron masks and the use of maggots in torture! Most teachers don't even know how to SPELL discipline let alone dish it out! It's pathetic. What DO they teach them at Teacher Training College these days?

Thankfully there are plenty of gruesome grown-ups in the support services. Librarians, for example, are made of much sterner stuff. It's all that reading they do. It fires their imaginations and gives them evil ideas! Take Dolly and Dot. They taught me everything I know about cataloguing. And I don't mean filing books. I mean nailing a cat to a log and pushing it down a river!

Oh, happy days!

SILENCE IS GOLDEN

Dolly and Dot were sisters first and school librarians second. They were gentle and grey-haired on the outside, but inside – underneath that sheen of carbolic, behind that puff of talcum powder, beyond the boiled sweets, the tissues and the tears shed for every dead dog – *inside*, Dolly and Dot were as twisted as a whelk-winkler's knife!

You can generally tell what a lady is like from the contents of her handbag.

If you don't believe me, take a gander at 'Her Majesty's Moley' on page 69 . . .

Dolly and Dot never left home without tissues and a lipstick, a telescopic blowpipe, a knotted silk garrotte and a vial of deadly poison extracted from the throat of the Slimy Green Toad of Tahiti!

They worked in the library of a school in Colchester, where the children were so noisy that a herd of flat-footed elephants in

pink tutus could have danced past the building and nobody inside would have heard them.

Granted, *all* children are noisy (they only have two settings on their voice boxes: *full on* or *full off*) but the children at this school were so noisy that the teachers had to wear ear plugs to stop their ear drums from bleeding.

* * *

It was all because of one girl. Her name was Dolores Bellicose. She had a voice so loud she could stop a pack of greedy third-formers at twenty paces, which is exactly what happened in the playground after Tuesday Tuck Shop, when a gang of twelve of them, led by a foolhardy girl called Tiggy the Specs, had her Crew creep up on Dolores's bag of mint imperials with a view to pinching them. It would have worked, except one of them stood on a snail.

Dolores heard the crunch, span round and fired off her mouth like a machine gun. 'DON'T EVEN THINK ABOUT EATING MY SWEETS!' she bellowed.

The blast from her voice knocked the third-formers off their feet with the force of a hurricane,

and deposited Tiggy the Specs on top of the science block roof.

It was because Dolores's voice was so loud that every other child in the school had to shout to be heard over her. This was what made this school in Colchester the noisiest in the world. For example, at lunchtime, a simple request like 'Pass the ketchup' would cause major structural damage to the dining room with sound waves registering twelve on the Richter scale.

'PASS THE KETCHUP!' That was Dolores.

Meanwhile Pete Tinker, who was sitting close to Dolores and was only trying to save his chips from the grasping fingers of Robbie Glottle, had to raise the level of *his* voice to remonstrate with the chip thief. 'OI! THOSE WERE *MY* CHI—'

But Dolores still hadn't got her ketchup, because nobody had heard her above Robbie. So *she* had to step up a notch too. 'PASS THE KETCHUP!'

Which meant that Robbie couldn't hear what Pete was saying.

'WHAT DID YOU SAY?' Pete repeated what he'd said by hollering back to Robbie.

'THOSE WERE *MY* CHI-'

Only to have his words drowned out again by an impatient Dolores. 'PASS THE KETCHUP!'

'I CAN'T HEAR YOU,' Robbie yelled to Pete.

'PASS THE KETCHUP!'

'NOT YOU *HIM!*,' Robbie bawled at Dolores.

'WHAT DID YOU SAY?' screamed Pete, who now thought that Dolores had been shouting at him all along and he just hadn't heard.

'KETCHUP!'

screeched Dolores. It was this particular word that broke all decibel records in the United Kingdom, shook the building to its core and plunged the dining hall into silence. And it was during this brief lull that the hurt voice of Pete Tinker finally made itself heard.

'There's no need to shout,' he said.

But there was. Dolores loved shouting. If she shouted loud enough it meant that *hers* was the only voice ever heard. It meant that everyone else

had to stop talking and listen to what she was saying, which made her the most important person in the room. And the room in which she liked shouting best was, of course, the library, where silence was the golden rule and her voice sounded twice as loud as anywhere else in the school.

I love school rules, because children are always breaking them. And when they do it's my rules that take over. RULE NUMBER ONE – Dead or Alive! I'll take you any which way I can!

* * *

It was on a Thursday that Dolores finally sealed her fate. She was late for her first lesson, which was Library. Without her there the rest of the class had no need to shout, so the first ten minutes passed in peaceful silence with everyone reading their books. At ten past nine the door burst open and Dolores entered like a whirlwind.

'WOTCHA!' she screamed as she spat her chewing gum into the dustbin. Dolly and Dot looked up from their novels and sighed.

'You're late,' said Dot.

'IT'S NOT MY FAULT!' bellowed the

girl. 'SO WOULD YOU HAVE BEEN IF YOU'D HAD A JOURNEY IN LIKE MINE!'

'Dolores,' said Dolly firmly. 'Sit down. We're trying to read our—'

'I HAVEN'T TOLD YOU WHAT HAPPENED ON MY JOURNEY YET!'

It was Dot's turn to try. 'Save it till later,' she said, but Dolores ignored her.

'I WAS ON THE BUS, RIGHT, SHOUTING INTO THE EAR OF THIS *SELFISH* OLD MAN WHO WAS SITTING IN MY SEAT. "GET UP, GRANDAD," I YELLED. "GIVE UP YOUR SEAT FOR A LADY!"'

Dot tried again. 'Dolores, please!' But she got the same result.

'AND WHEN HE WOULDN'T GET UP, I SCREAMED TILL HE DID. LIKE THIS. *AAAAAAAAAAAAAAAAAAGH!*'

Dolly tried to interrupt. 'Dolores!'

'BUT, GET THIS, MY SCREAM SMASHED THE WINDSCREEN AND WE CRASHED INTO A HERD OF ELEPHANTS IN PINK TUTUS DANCING DOWN THE STREET!'

At that point Tamara Tapeworm joined in. This

was significant, because the introduction of another voice jacked up the level. 'I SAW THE ELEPHANTS TOO,' she cried.

'Children!' trilled Dot, trying to keep a lid on it, but the stew was out of the pot.

'ME TOO!' shouted Pankot Chumbawumba.

'AND ME!' bawled Barry Pew.

'AND ME!'

'AND ME!'

'AND ME!'

'Will everyone stop shouting!' Dolly tried to raise her voice to top the swelling noise, but didn't get close.

'DOESN'T ANYONE WANT TO HEAR WHAT HAPPENED AFTER THE CRASH?' hollered Dolores, thrusting herself back into the limelight.

'Quiet!' squeaked the two old ladies together. But even together their voices were no match for Dolores.

'QUIET YOURSELF!' roared the decibel queen. 'YOU TWO MAKE MORE NOISE THAN THE REST OF US PUT TOGETHER! HA HA HA!' And the whole class followed suit. When the class

started laughing, Dolly and Dot knew that they had lost. 'HEY! LET'S TURN THE LIGHTS OUT!' yelled Dolores. 'THEN IT'S MORE LIKE READING IN BED.'

'YEAAAAAH!' came the mob's reply. As the lights went out all over the library, Dolly and Dot beat a retreat, leaving the children to scream until they were sick.

What did you say? Speak up! I can't hear you...

But we can hear YOU, Jumbo! And rather wish we couldn't.

***

There is only so far you can push a librarian. And on this particular occasion, Dolly and Dot had been pushed **BEYOND THE POINT OF . . .**

NO REVENGE!

Dolly and Dot slumped into a couple of wobbly chairs in the cubbyhole that was laughingly referred to as their office. Dolly handed Dot a pair of scissors then removed the copy of *The Poisoner's Bible* from the top of the glass tank behind her head and handed her sister the crocodile.

'Oh, Dolly!' said Dot, as she clipped the crocodile's toenails.

'Oh, Dot,' said Dolly. 'Why won't they listen to us?'

'Because they can't hear what we're saying over Dolores, dear. We need to shut her up—' an evil thought flitted through her mind '—for good!'

'Ooh, Dot. I've just had an idea,' gasped Dolly, breathing out onto a brass knuckleduster and polishing it on her cardigan. 'Why don't we break Dolores into bits and file her away under T for tongue and F for foot . . . No, no, no! Even better! Nobody ever goes into the Ancient History section, we could file *all* of her in there.'

'Not sure that's such a good idea, Dolly dear. I think the police might want a word with us.'

'Quite right,' said Dolly. 'We wouldn't want to do anything illegal.'

'No, dear.' Dot took a moment to replace the crocodile in the tank and feed the tarantula. Then she pushed her teeth out through her lips and sucked them back into place with a slurp. 'What we need,' she said cunningly, 'is the help of an alchemist.'

'An alchemist?' said Dolly.

'A wizard who can turn things to gold.'

'Gold! Gosh!' Dolly was impressed. 'Why?'

'Because,' said Dot mysteriously, 'silence is golden.'

'Oh very good,' smiled Dolly, replacing the knuckleduster on the desk next to the eye-gouge. 'Very good indeed.'

It's a strange thing about eye gouges – now you see them, now you don't!

The two old ladies looked up 'Alchemist' in the *Yellow-Gold Pages* and found an evil genius on a quiet trading estate in Billerickie. 'Quiet' was perfect for what Dolly and Dot had in mind, and evil genius wasn't bad either.

Aaaaaaaaaaaagh! This is a nightmare!

A bit of quiet wouldn't be bad, either!

The alchemist's name was Dr Calf. 'Bring her here to the laboratory and I'll do the necessary,' he said coldly, when the librarians had explained their problem. 'Anything else?'

'Well, yes,' said Dolly. 'What shall we do with Dolores once we've turned her into gold?'

'Good question,' said Dot. 'It seems a shame to waste her, doesn't it? Maybe, just for a change, we should turn her into something *useful*.'

'We could always melt her down into a necklace,' squeaked Dolly-the-psycho. Dot furrowed her brow. 'You know, Dolly dear, there is a cruel streak to you that I've never noticed before.'

'Is there, dear? Does it shock you?'

'Not at all,' laughed Dot. 'I like it!'

'We could always sell her.'

'And make money out of her. Yes! We could fund a little Silence Project for the library.'

'My word, what a splendid idea,' cried Dolly, 'a Silence Project. What perfect irony!'

'I'll have a word with some museum people I know in Mexico,' said Dr Calf, who was waiting to gold-plate a gerbil. 'We can flog her off as an old Aztec statue. Good day.' Then he steered the librarians out of his laboratory and sent them on their way.

* * *

Somehow Dolly and Dot had to get Dolores into Dr. Calf's laboratory without raising her suspicions. They decided that going by bus would be the best option as they could use their Over-60s bus passes and it wouldn't cost them a penny.

***

The following Monday, on the pavement outside school, they separated Dolores from her friends with the help of a well-aimed wheelchair. Dolores had just said goodbye to everyone – 'BYE, EVERYONE!' – and stunned several pigeons out of a tree, when a runaway wheelchair caught her a stinging blow on the back of the knees. The force of it caused her knees to buckle and she had to sit down, whereupon the wheelchair whizzed her to the edge of the pavement, tipped up in the gutter and propelled her into a bus, where Dolly and Dot were waiting for her. They were slightly out of breath, having first given the wheelchair a shove, then run past it in order to be on the bus before Dolores arrived. She landed in the empty seat between them.

'Oh, there you are, dear,' said Dot, as if Dolores's

appearance was no surprise at all.

'ARE YOU TWO KIDNAPPING ME?' screamed the girl, trying to draw attention to herself.

'Ssssh,' whispered Dolly. 'Don't be silly, dear.'

'Do we look like desperadoes?' giggled Dot.

'BECAUSE IF YOU *ARE*,' persisted the world's loudest mouth, 'I SHALL SCREAM!'

'Not again, please!' begged the bus driver, brushing the remains of a pink dancing dress out of his face. It was snagged in a crack in his windscreen. 'I am still peering through this elephant's tutu from this morning!'

'No, dear. No!' said Dot. 'We're not kidnapping you. We're taking you to see a doctor friend of ours to measure the loudness of that pretty little voice of yours.'

'WHY?'

'Because,' said Dolly slowly, giving herself time to invent a good lie, 'we think you should be in the *Guinness Book of World Records*.' Dolores was impressed.

'*THE GUINNESS BOOK OF WORLD RECORDS*! BUT I'LL BE FAMOUS!'

'Yes, so we don't want you wasting your voice by screaming now. Understood?' Dolores nodded her head.

'Good girl!' said Dolly, flashing a sinister smile.

***

Once inside Dr. Calf's laboratory Dolores continued this run of good behaviour by saying very little. It probably had something to do with the straps around her jaw and the tin-plated helmet delivering 16,000 volts through her brain. Dolly and Dot heard an 'Ooh!' and an 'Ow!' and one final 'Ugh!' as the frothing girl was turned into gold. Then there was silence.

Later that night, a wooden box was dragged out through a back door of the laboratory and loaded on to a tractor. It was driven to the coast, where a merchant ship bound for Mexico City was waiting to depart. The box was loaded into the hold and the captain handed over a large wad of cash to the delivery team – two sweet old ladies and an alchemist.

And there the story should have ended, had the merchant ship not been hijacked by a band of cut-throat pirates, two of which had remarkably smooth skin for old seadogs. They had only just joined the ship under the names Dead-Eyed Dot and Dolly

Dogbreath. Anyway, during the transfer of the golden statue to their ship these two pirates, who had been ordered to hold on tight to the safety rope, 'accidentally' let it slip, and the statue plunged into the water.

'Whoops!' cried Dead-Eyed Dot. 'Butter fingers!' But it was too late to do anything about it. Hundreds of feet beneath the surface of the water, Dolores Bellicose was sinking like a silent stone.

She came to rest on the sea bed, where she still stands today, where not a strand of her golden hair moves in the current, where sharks brush past her metal skin, where an octopus sleeps on her head and where nobody, even if she could open her mouth, will ever hear her scream.

You won't be surprised to know that the school in Colchester isn't noisy any more. In fact the silence in the school library is more silent than the silence in the library of a Trappist Monastery. There's a good reason for this. Fear.

After their holiday, Dolly and Dot came back with one or two new ideas for their Silence Project. Now, if anyone talks in the library, or squeaks or burps or even *looks* like they might make a noise,

Dolly and Dot simply open the window and make them walk the plank.

Does the trick every time!

It's such a shame that I never got my hands on Dolores. I had her room ready and everything. It was a sound-proofed cell filled with round-the-clock ear pain: the cry of a hungry baby, the squeak of a piece of chalk scraped down a blackboard and the whine of a high-speed dentist's drill!

I expect I'll get letters of complaint now from dentists. Well, they can write as many as they like. I shan't reply. I don't write letters anymore. Not after I wrote one to that popular magazine that caters for badly dressed people who wear offensive clothing TANK TOP WEEKLY! and never got a reply.

Boo hoo hoo! Boo hoo hoo!

I hope that's not sarcasm, Poppy.

THE HOTHELL DARKNESS

Friday 35th

Dear Tank Top Weekly!

It is high time someone asked the unaskable question. Can the elimination of a child for displaying an offensive taste in clothes ever be justified? In my opinion, the answer is a resounding YES. Today's children are too vain. They care far too much about what they look like. It's all 'OOH! LOOK AT ME, EVERYONE! I'M A REBEL. I'M SO COOL, BECAUSE I LOOK DIFFERENT FROM EVERYONE ELSE!' Well, take it from me, any child striving to look different generally ends up looking a MESSY MINGER! To this end I would recommend to you The Old Tailor of Pelting Moor who has helped me out more times than I care to mention. He is a uniquely evil old man who takes enormous pride in his work – namely stitching up vain children – and I cannot recommend him highly enough to your readership.
Yours etc etc

PS Obviously, etc etc is NOT my name. My name is a closely guarded secret. If I told your readership my name I would have to kill each and every one of them, and as your readership is in excess of three and a half million this might prove rather time consuming.

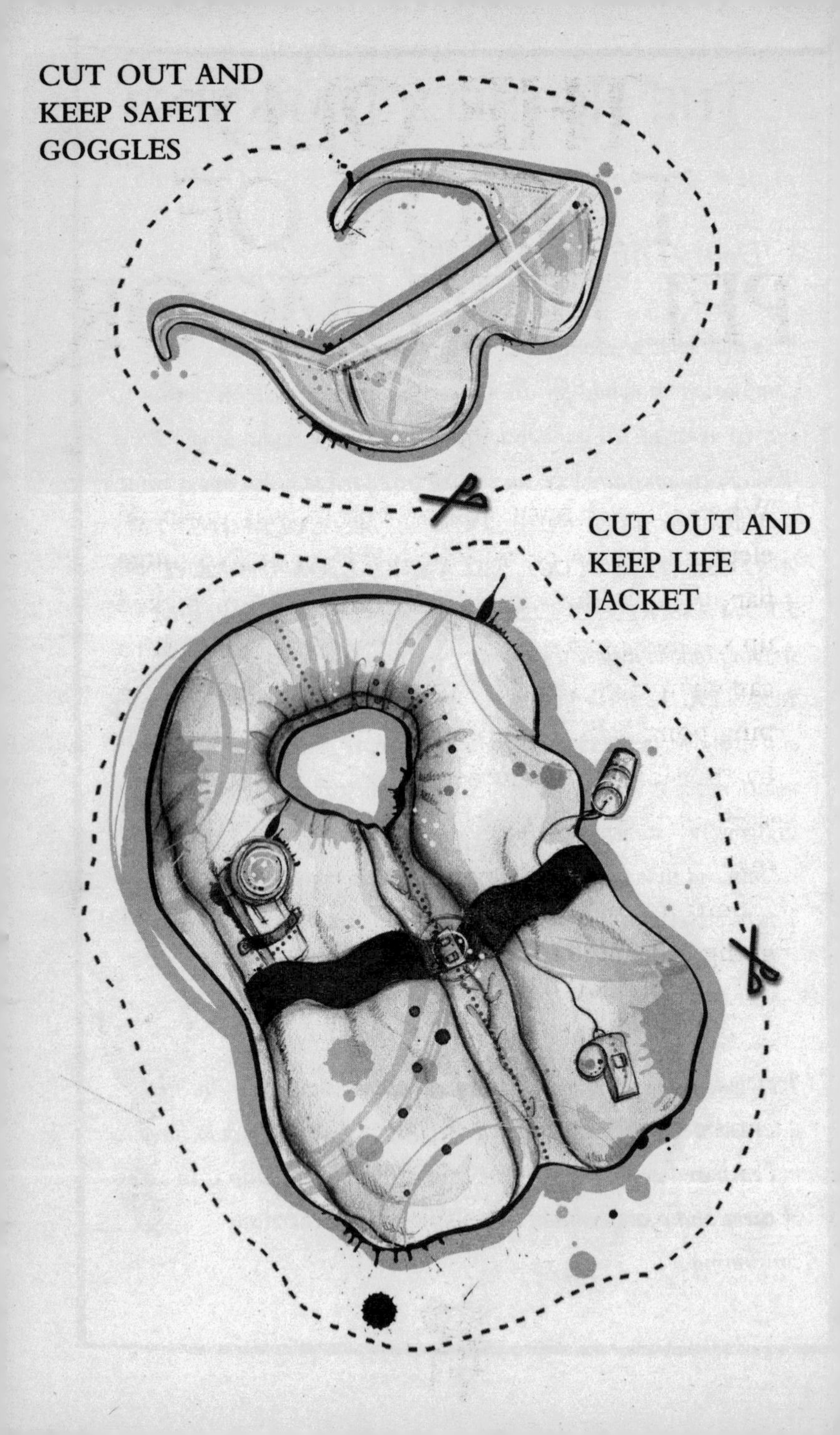
CUT OUT AND
KEEP SAFETY
GOGGLES
CUT OUT AND
KEEP LIFE
JACKET

THE OLD TAILOR OF PELTING MOOR

When he was born, Jumbo Ferrari was given an elephant's name, because he had big ears. Not huge flapping ears that caught in swing doors or picked up satellite signals, but ears that were big enough to cast their own shadow and frighten the life out of ping pong balls. While he was still a baby in his cot by the side of his mother's hospital bed he caught sight of these ears reflected in a kidney bowl and made a life-changing decision.

Those are such big ears, he thought, that I'm never going to be able to hide them with hair. I'm going to have to think of some other form of distraction to take peoples' attention away from them. His distraction of choice was clothes. He would wear clothes that were so outrageous and bizarre that nobody would notice his ears.

The following morning he threw the hospital blanket out of his cot and made it clear, by refusing to be wrapped in it again, that he did not want to wear the same as other babies. He only stopped crying when they wrapped him up in newspaper; so that was how he left to go home. By the time he was out of nappies, he would only wear clothes that did NOT go together – swimming costumes and Wellington boots, baggy shorts and long johns, frilly shirts and tank top jumpers. No item of clothing was taboo, so long as it made him look different from other children and distracted from his ears. He bought blouses from clothes shops for girls, four-legged coats designed for afghan hounds and dead peoples' clothes from the charity shop. He clashed colours and styles, while experimenting with hats and divers' boots, plastic macs and jewellery and sheepskin socks with tartan trousers. But above all, he gained a reputation for looking like the scary geek to avoid on the bus!

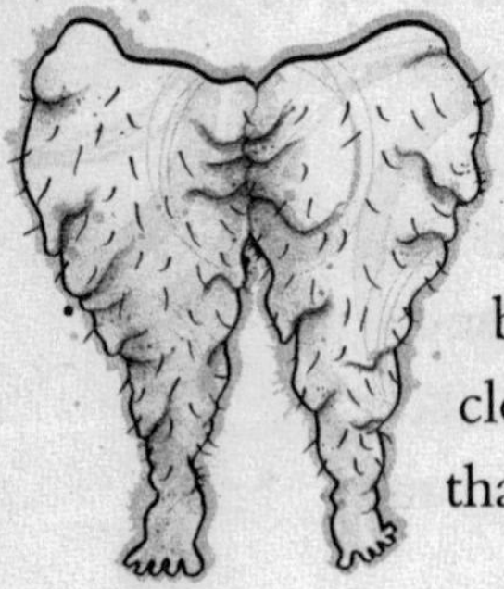

By the time he was eleven, however, what had started off as ear-distraction had turned into full-blown vanity. His bizarre style of clothing was more important to him than anything else in the world. As far as he was concerned, he was living his life at the cutting edge of fashion.

It wore his poor parents out.

Helpful Hints on How To Deal With Gruesome Grown-ups

2. WORN-OUT PARENTS

Worn out parents are not a problem. They can be darned. Find a sturdy needle and thread, then visit www.darnedparents.com and ask to see their catalogue.

In fact they were so worn-out that strangers who saw them on the street thought that they were Jumbo's grandparents. It was the grey hair, stooping shoulders and bungee cords of spit that bounced up and down from the corners of their mouths.

'Have you any idea how much all of these clothes cost us?' croaked Jumbo's mum one morning, when Jumbo walked into breakfast wearing an edible boiler suit trimmed with fake leopard fur, a pink rope belt and a gold baseball cap with the word GEEZER stitched across the front.

'Mama,' he replied, in the poor French accent that he'd cultivated to complement his image, 'when you are as big a fashion icon as *moi*, cost is an irritating irrelevancy!'

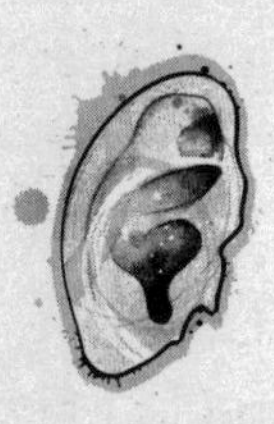

'To you maybe, but not to us!' grumbled his father, who was using a piece of burnt toast to black in the scuff marks on his shoes. 'Have you noticed by any chance that we don't have a bedroom?'

'You don't *need* a bedroom,' laughed Jumbo. 'You got it right first time when you made me. Why go through all that palaver again?'

'We haven't got a bedroom, because it's full of your clothes!' coughed his mother, clasping a stained, yellow handkerchief to her prunish lips. 'They're Piled up in front of the window. I haven't seen a sunrise for six years.'

'And whose fault is that?' cried Jumbo. 'Not mine. Buy a bigger house with an extra wing for my clothes and you can have your bedroom back.'

'You've spent all our money,' wheezed his father, returning to his favourite topic.

'So you'd have me going out in public looking like a chav?' cried Jumbo. 'It costs money to be one of life's beautiful people,' he added modestly. 'An expense, however, that is paid back by the many admiring glances I attract in the street.' To call them admiring glances was not strictly accurate. They were looks of utter, jaw-dropping disbelief.

There was no arguing with Jumbo's vanity. He was obsessed by how he looked. Clothes were obviously important, but so was his hair, which was restyled every fortnight; his moisturising routine, which included full nasal waxing and mud packs; and his freckles, which he bought from the Flipping Frinton Freckle Factory and stuck on every morning!

Whenever his parents pointed out that a life spent in thrall to vanity was a pointless and ultimately wasted life, Jumbo struck back with vitriol.

'At least I don't look like you two,' he said. 'Better to be vain than old and ugly!' His parents had never paid much attention to their clothes, even less now that they could not afford to buy them. They made do with practical brown cardigans and comfortable slippers, grey housecoats and slacks, or matching

fawn anoraks with double-strength zips. They cut out the cold with car coats and warm woolly hats and preferred their colours dull to blend in with their dull lives. Their dress sense was exactly the opposite of Jumbo's, which is why he despised them.

But to despise one's own parents is a very dangerous game to play, because parents are programmed to correct the faults that they find in their children. They have no choice. It is the Grown-Up way. Jumbo's parents knew only one way to correct their son's vanity. They picked up the phone and made a person to person call: PELTING MOOR 4606.

I'm going to treat you to one of my famous songs now. Lucky you.

> Kids who hate their parents
> They are bad, bad, bad.
> Falling out of love
> With their mum and dad.
> If the way they look annoys
> And gets underneath your skin,
> Then the only cure I know
> Is to change the skin you're in!

***

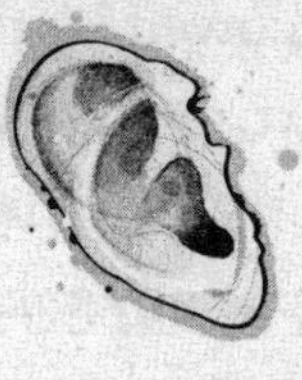
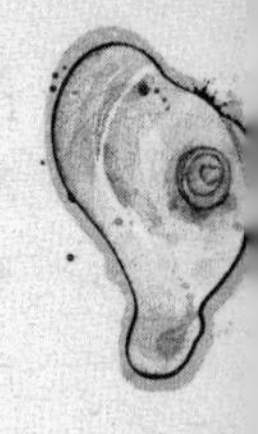

It was no coincidence, therefore, that two weeks after this conversation with his parents, Jumbo saw an advertisement in a fashion magazine for a new type of suit.

> The Unique Life Suit
>
> The latest in bespoke craftsmanship from the Old Tailor of Pelting Moor

Every suit was tailored to the individual so it was different from every other suit ever made in the world. Jumbo *had* to have one. He scoured the page, but there was no contact address, no phone number and surprisingly no Pelting Moor on the map. So he tucked the advertisement under his pillow with the intention of tracking down the Old Tailor in the morning.

But that night he had a dream. In his dream, he was asleep in bed when he heard a noise in his wardrobe. It sounded like old bones rattling,

followed by the flapping of leathery wings. Not the sort of noise you particularly want to investigate in the middle of the night, especially when the light switch is on the other side of the room. But, being a dream, in which the dreamer never does what common sense dictates, Jumbo got out of bed and opened the wardrobe door.

Slowly, of course . . .

Inch by inch . . .

Only to be knocked flat by the door bursting open and his beloved clothes jumping out! They stamped all over him as they danced across his bedroom like an invisible boy band, opened the window and threw themselves out. He rushed over to see where they'd landed, but there was no sign of them. His clothes had vanished and the cupboard was bare!

* * *

Jumbo woke with a start. He was sweating all over. The thought of losing his beautiful clothes was enough to paralyse his heart! He gulped in a large pocket of air as a wooden groan span his eyes to the wardrobe. What he saw there made his pupils dilate.

'My clothes!' he wailed. 'Give me back my precious clothes!' It had been much more than just a dream. His wardrobe *was* bare.

Unable to believe his own eyes, Jumbo stumbled into the wardrobe to check for false bottoms and sides, but as he fell against the back panel, it gave way. It collapsed backwards under his weight and swung through the wall like a door. Jumbo fell through the hole into the shadows of a dark and silent room.

Buckle up! Here comes the gruesome grown-up!

It was a tailor's basement workshop. Through the narrow high windows on the back wall, Jumbo could see the faint shapes of legs walking along a pavement. The glass was grimy black and choked out the sunlight. The only lighting, therefore, came from two candles that flickered on the large central table and threw the boiling shadow of a man on to the ceiling. Between the candles, as yet oblivious to the stranger watching him, sat a cross-legged old man sewing a piece of cloth. He had a bald head crowned by white, wispy hair, thick spectacles and a thimble on his finger. He also had the droopiest, flappiest, wrinkliest skin that Jumbo had ever seen. It hung off his bones like an old turkey's wattle.

'Ah,' he said suddenly, raising his red eyes. 'Is that Mr Ferrari? Welcome.'

'Who are you?' said Jumbo, still hugging the floor, as if somehow the flagstones were going to protect him from this wizened walnut of a man.

'The Old Tailor of Pelting Moor at your service, sir.'

'How did I get here?' asked Jumbo, cautiously.

'Never ask *how*,' winked the old man, easing himself achingly off his perch. 'The question is always *why*. You're here, my dear sir, for a life suit.' He slid open a drawer in one of the tall cabinets at the side of the table. 'Allow me to show you a demonstration one.'

He pulled out an all-in-one jumpsuit which, quite literally, jumped to attention and brushed itself down in front of Jumbo. It was made from one

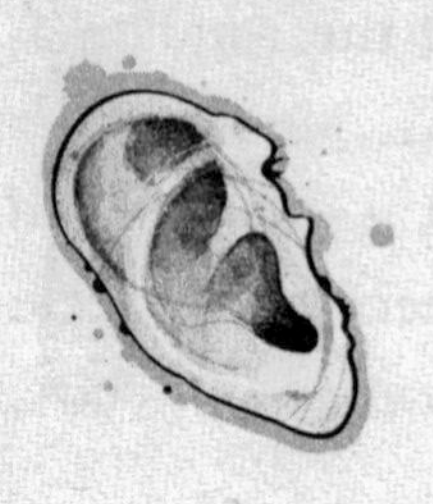  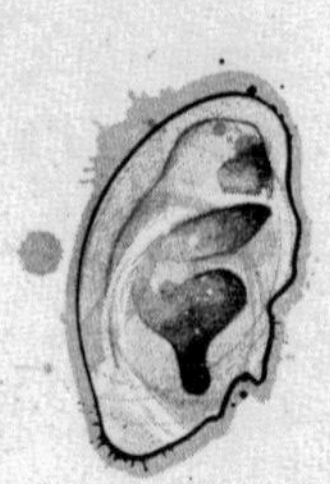

piece of cloth that shimmered like mother of pearl. A single cut it may have been, but it had been exquisitely tailored to look like a suit with a shirt underneath and separate jacket and trousers. Jumbo fell in love with it almost at once and couldn't stop himself from reaching out to touch it. 'Be my guest,' said the wrinkled tailor, reading Jumbo's mind.

He invited Jumbo to try the life suit on. 'It's beautiful,' said the boy.

'And not another like it in the world.'

That was what Jumbo wanted to hear. With his own personal life suit he'd be one of a kind!

* * *

The material hugged his body in a way that no other material had ever done before.

'It's so light,' gasped Jumbo. 'It's as if I wasn't wearing anything at all.'

The tailor laughed. 'Some people do say it's like wearing a second skin,' he said, brushing a small sprinkling of dandruff off the collar of the suit. There followed a short period of silence while Jumbo gazed adoringly at his reflection in a cracked mirror. During this pause the old tailor moved behind Jumbo to smooth down

the back of the life suit. As he took his first step, however, he tripped over the skin on his legs, which had collapsed over his ankles like a baggy old pair of woollen tights.

Jumbo paid no attention as the old man struggled back to his feet. Instead he smiled and said, 'It makes me handsome!'

Suddenly, in the mirror, the face of a complete stranger flitted across his own. It happened so quickly that Jumbo questioned whether he had seen it at all. 'Who was that?'

'Who?' said the tailor distractedly.

'The boy whose face just flashed across mine.'

'Oh, him,' said the old man. 'That was nobody. Just the face of the boy I made the suit from.'

'Made it *from*?'

'*For!* Made it *for*! Goodness me! Slip of an old man's tongue! So—' he added, steering off the subject quickly '—does sir want me to make him a life suit of his own?'

'Yes,' grinned Jumbo. 'Sir *does*!'

***

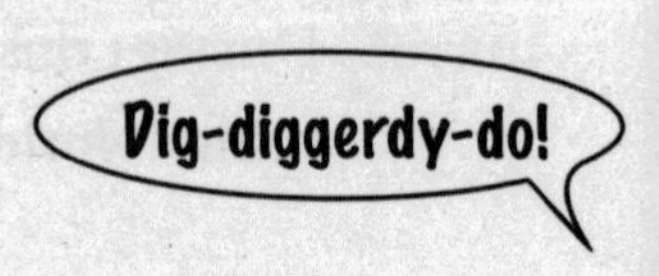

I won't tell you about the noise again, Mattie. If you want me to get the big spade out, I can!

The Old Tailor of Pelting Moor measured Jumbo from head to toe then politely asked him to step out of his skin.

'I beg your pardon?' chuckled the boy, thinking that this was an old tailor's joke.

'Did I not mention it?' mumbled the old man. He seemed distressed. 'Old age is such a curse. If it's not more wrinkles, it's less memory. Now, where was I? Oh yes. The reason why the life suit is unique is because it's made from the wearer's own skin.' Jumbo suddenly realised what that meant. 'So that face was the face of the boy whose skin I was wearing?'

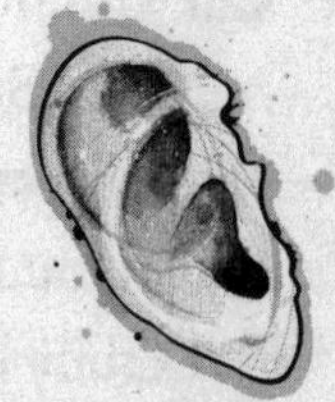

'Alas poor Yorick, I knew him well! It's a time-honoured process. First, I strip off the skin, which is lovingly preserved in unguents and oils to prevent ageing. Then I nip and I tuck and I might even snip a bit too to achieve the final look.'

'You're a plastic surgeon,' said Jumbo.

'Hardly, sir. The most skilful tailor in the world.' There was a flash of fury in

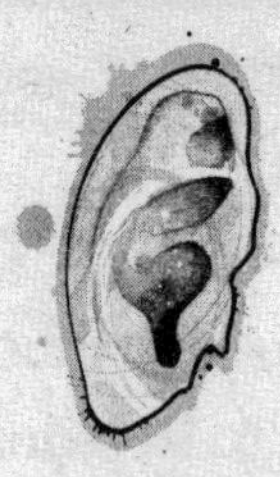

those rheumy eyes that Jumbo thought not to challenge.

'Very well,' he said, ignoring the side of his brain that was flagging up danger. 'And how exactly do I step out of my skin?'

'That is why we have ears, sir – in your case, quite large ones – to hide the carbon fibre poppers. Hold still and I'll have you out of there in a jiffy.' Then he leaned forward, popped off Jumbo's ears and revealed two red tags underneath. Each had a tiny label attached – **PULL TO RELEASE** - which is exactly what the old tailor did. Two sharp tugs and Jumbo stepped out of his skin like a work-experience ghost lifting off its white sheet.

All that night, Jumbo sat up in a chair in his bedroom and listened through the holes in the side of his skull to the old tailor working in the wardrobe. He wrapped a blanket around his shoulders to keep himself warm, for without a skin Jumbo was nothing more than a collection of bones, and cold draughts like nothing more

than ribs to whistle through.

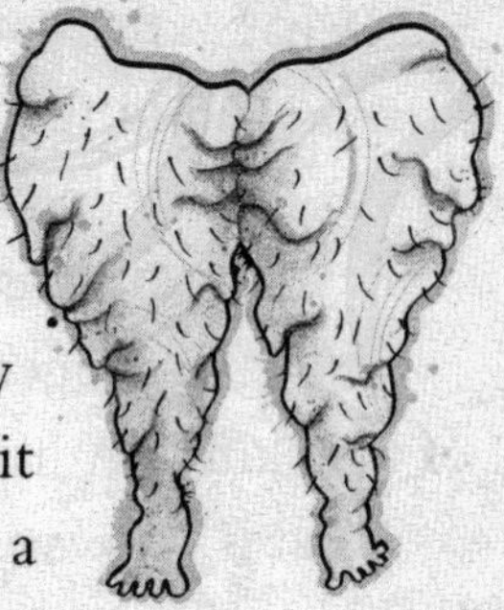

In the morning, Jumbo could barely contain his excitement as he and his bones clattered into the wardrobe to try on his Life Suit. He saw it immediately, hanging loosely on a peg, but the old tailor was nowhere to be seen. Without asking permission, Jumbo tried it on.

'Good morning, sir. How does it fit?' asked a familiar voice from behind him. Jumbo neither replied nor turned round, for at that precise moment he was popping back his second ear and lifting his head to admire his new suit in the mirror. As his eyes hit the glass he gasped and clutched his mouth. In his worst nightmares he had never imagined it looking like *this*.

The suit was appallingly made. It bore no resemblance to the demonstration model he'd been shown. The trousers were ragged shorts, the jacket covered less shoulder than a scarf and the shirt looked like a stretched, overworn T-shirt. And hanging out from beneath the clothes were folds and folds and folds of old man's skin. Loose and drooping, saggy and wrinkled!

'What have you *done* to me?' howled Jumbo, turning round to confront the old tailor – but the shocks just kept coming, because the tailor wasn't old any more. He had young, firm skin and fine, chiselled features. Admittedly, he had only one ear, but everything else about the old tailor looked radiantly youthful. 'That's my skin!' stammered Jumbo. 'You're wearing my skin, and I'm wearing . . .' He looked down at his flapping body and burst into tears. 'These hideous wrinkles!' he cried. 'You've turned me into you!'

'It's not so bad,' smiled the tailor. 'You'll get used to tripping over the folds of skin when you walk downstairs. Word of advice, though – if you go cycling, you'll need to hitch the wrinkles up above your knees with bicycle clips, and don't go outside in a bathing costume if there's a high wind. Your arm skin will inflate like bat wings and you'll take off.'

Jumbo could not believe what he was hearing. 'But apart from that,' added the tailor, 'your life won't be that much different.'

'Won't be different!' choked Jumbo. 'You're an old crook! You've stolen my beauty!'

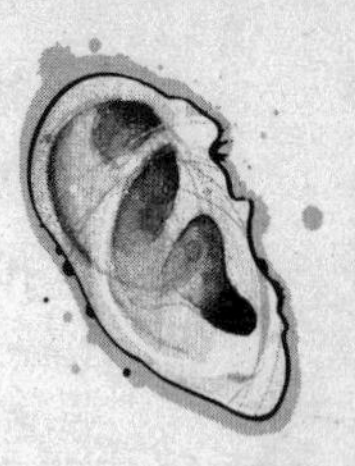

'Precisely,' said the tailor without a hint of a smile. 'Vanity in one so young deserves wrinkles. And at my great age, I rather think I deserve a facelift!'

Oh, he is good!

And with that, the *young* tailor of Pelting Moor took his other ear out of his pocket, pressed it on to the popper on the side of his skull and vanished, along with his workshop, leaving Jumbo Ferrari standing in the middle of his bedroom with no other option but to face the rest of his life wearing an old man's saggy, baggy skin!

From that day on, Jumbo went out in public only when he absolutely had to, but never to buy himself clothes. Cutting-edge fashion just didn't suit Jumbo any more. His parents, who suddenly had spare money to put aside for their old age, thoroughly approved of the change in their son.

'Not so chic now,' grinned his father.

'No,' sniggered his mother. 'Not with skin designed by Jumbo the Elephant!'

I'm glad to report that a few months later, Jumbo DID go out in a high wind wearing only a bathing costume and DID take off. He was up there for weeks, floating around the world on a Trade Wind. When he came down, he came down rather too hard, and made a hole so deep that he ended up on my doorstep.

I've put him in the Old Folk's Wing with other ancient children. It's rather sweet. The old dears have called it DUN LIVIN'. He's got his own room with his own coffin where the bed should be, and he spends his days sitting in a high-backed chair wearing a nice brown cardigan and comfortable slippers. And if he goes out he wraps up warm in a practical fawn anorak with a double-strength zip. Just like his father in fact! The father he once, rather foolishly, despised! What did you say? Speak up. I can't hear you!

Just listen to the old man go on. You go back to sleep, Jumbo. I'll be round in a minute with your medication.

Isn't it spooky the way children ALWAYS end up looking and behaving like their parents?

HER MAJESTY'S MOLEY

There was barely room to move. Certainly not backwards. The sides of the tunnel scraped every sinew of his body as he squirmed forward, coat damp and slick, blindly digging a path towards the perimeter. A noise up ahead made him stop and cock an ear. A soft thump, like a mouse falling on to dead leaves. But it wasn't a mouse. It was bigger than a mouse. It rolled towards him and bumped into his head. It was metal-hard with a pitted surface and a chain, which he nuzzled. Sniffing for a clue to its identity, he found the hole where the pin had once been. But that was all. As he flicked out his tongue to taste the object, it revealed itself in all its brutal horror. In a flash he was dispatched into a silent storm, splattered into a white hot furnace of oblivion.

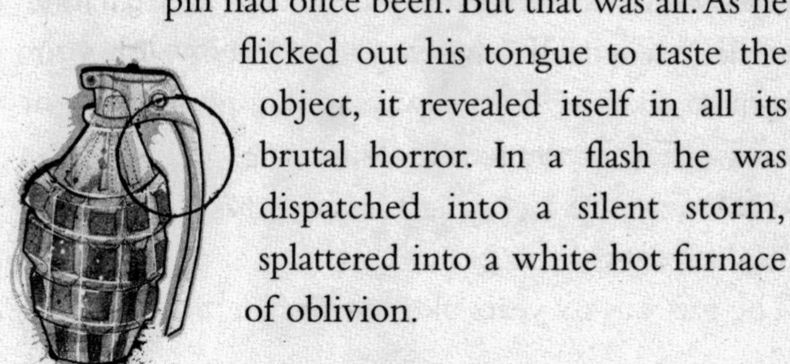

***

Don't eat me again! Please don't eat me again!

Ignore it. That's just the tiles talking!

'My turn! My turn!' squealed the little girl in the garden above. 'Can I drop a hand grenade into the mole's hole now?' She and her father were standing next to a smoking hole in a lawn that was blistered with molehills.

'No,' said her father. 'In a year or two. But, if I can just find the little blighter . . .' He knelt down, thrust his hand into the hole and, after fumbling around, produced the dead digger like a rabbit from a hat. 'There. If you want to hold it, I'll take your photograph.' Then he snapped away while the mole's battered body stained the grass red with its sticky drips. 'Say cheese!' her father cried. 'Smile!' The camera clicked. 'Now it's your turn to take me.' They always took a photograph of each other for the family album.

***

The girl was six years old, and wore a pinafore dress

and muddy red wellingtons. Her name was Mattie and ever since she'd been old enough to ask if she could join him, her father had taken her out on Mole Hunts. He was forty-eight years old, grey-haired and dressed for hunting – rifle over his shoulder, spade in hand and a quiver strapped across his back with rockets poking out.

Mattie and her father were like two peas in a pod. They both loved killing moles. To be fair, a hand grenade was not Mattie's father's preferred weapon of mole destruction. It was just that on this particular morning, he had happened to find one in the potting shed.

Normally, he and Mattie would leave home early in the morning before the moles were awake, drop loudspeakers down their holes and pump Drum and Bass through the tunnels until the moles were driven mad by the noise and ran out clutching their ears. Then he'd bash them on the head with a spade.

'Me next! Me next!' Mattie shouted keenly every time, but her father drew the line at spade work.

'It's too violent for a little girl like you, Mattie. Have a rocket instead.'

And so it was, from an early age, that Mattie

became expert at positioning firework rockets in mole holes, lighting the blue touch paper and retiring, safe in the knowledge that when you put a rocket up a mole there tends to only ever be one winner.

***

On this particular morning however, having slung the grenade-splattered mole on the compost heap, Mattie was handed her first rocket of the day and told to 'Go bag another!'

Unfortunately, her rocket missed its mark. Instead of killing its intended target it caught the mole a glancing blow and maimed it instead. When Mattie's father reached into the hole to pull out the body all he found was a severed front paw. 'Never mind,' he said, consoling his weeping daughter. 'You won't miss every time! Let's see if we can't make something special out of this.' And he took the paw back to his potting shed and turned it into a souvenir key-ring.

'Keep this always, Mattie,' he said, stooping onto one knee and pressing the keyring into her tiny hand. 'Let it be a permanent reminder of our

mole-mangling days together.'

'Oh I shall, daddy,' she wept. 'I shall call it Moley and whenever I stroke its soft, silky fur I shall remember all the blood we've spilled together!'

What neither of them realised was that the poor owner of the paw was still very much alive and had limped to the hole of a mole doctor – that's doctor as in *witch* not *medicine* – and knocked on his door. The mole was holding his injured paw across his chest and breathing heavily when the door was opened by an elderly mole wearing a grass skirt and spectacles. He had a feathered necklace around his neck, bracelets of teeth around his wrists and a small bone through his nose.

'Good morning,' he said in a well-to-do tone. 'How may I help you? Exorcism, curse, voodoo doll or haunting?'

The three-pawed mole came to the point. 'Do you do revenge?' he asked.

'Ooh yes,' said the doctor. 'I love a good revenge.'

'Excellent.'

'Do come in.'

'Thank you.' But the injured mole hesitated on the door step. Then, with an awkward forward thrust of his stump he mumbled apologetically, 'Normally I'd shake your hand, but I haven't . . . erm . . . Sorry.'

The witch doctor waved formality aside and took his visitor through to his witch surgery where they threw some magic bones and cursed cruel Mattie and her equally cruel father to a horrible end.

For those who have never come across such a thing before, the Curse of a Mole is rarely instantaneous. This meant that Mattie lived blissfully unaware of it and carried on blowing up moles without a care in the world until she was eleven years old. The curse kicked in on the day of her father's accident. He took a swing at a mole's head with his spade, missed and hit his foot.

'Nooooooooo!' she cried as she watched the leading metal edge slice through his combat boots. 'Daddddddddddddy!'

For his part, Mattie's father kept it short and sweet. 'Ow!' he said. 'That hurt.'

He died, three weeks later, from gangrene.

This was the end of the first part of the mole's revenge.

***

Two hundred million people watched his funeral. It was a bigger than average turnout, but then he was not just Mattie's father, he was the prime minister of Great Britain as well. The funeral was a sumptuous affair, televised across the globe in twenty-five different languages, with eulogies showered on his cold head by statesmen from the four corners of the earth.

This tale should really be called The Tale of Two Dead Paws, shouldn't it? You'll like this. Dead Paw Number 1 was the three-pawed mole's dead paw, which was blown off by a rocket. Dead Paw Number 2 was Mattie's dead paw, who was the prime minister. Gettit?

Mattie's father was greatly missed by everyone; everyone that is except moles; and one mole in particular. Old Three-Paws himself!

***

'Now,' he said, as he watched the late Prime Minister's coffin being lowered into the ground, 'let the second part of my revenge commence!'

'You're the boss!' said the witch doctor, draining his cup of tick-blood tea and switching off the television with the remote control. 'Hold this, will you?' He gave his cup to the three-pawed mole and squatted in the middle of the room. Then he closed his eyes and invoked the evil spirits of the Holy Moleland with a chant that he'd Googled off the internet. '*Humma hoinnng . . . oing . . . oing . . . oing!*'

When the witch doctor had finished chanting for the second part of the mole's revenge, the three-pawed mole left to do his duty.

'Are you sure you know the way?' asked the witch doctor. 'I've got an Underground map on the shelf somewhere.'

'No need,' said the three-pawed mole. 'I should be able to find Downing Street with my eyes closed.'

'And you're sure you know what the key-ring looks like?'

'It is *my* paw,' said Old Three-Paws. 'See you later.' And he waved goodbye with his stump.

'Cheerio,' said his fellow conspirator. 'And good luck!'

* * *

It was only after the funeral was over and the guests had filed out of 10 Downing Street that Mattie noticed it was missing. She was clearing up the house with her mother when she spotted that the trinket box under her bed was empty!

'Someone's stolen my precious Moley!' she cried. 'What will I sniff when I suck my thumb now?' The house was turned upside down, but the mole's paw key-ring could not be found. After one whole hour of searching, her mother took Mattie to one side and whispered something secret in her ear.

'After the speeches,' she said, 'I was coming upstairs to find Elton John – I was going to ask him to sing us another sad song – when I saw someone slipping out of your room.'

'The thief!' gasped Mattie. 'Who was it?'

Her mother looked around nervously. 'The Queen,' she hissed. 'Now, I know that the royal family is having to make big changes to keep up with the times, but I don't believe she's changed into a burglar. I mean, generally speaking, queens aren't that interested in stealing.'

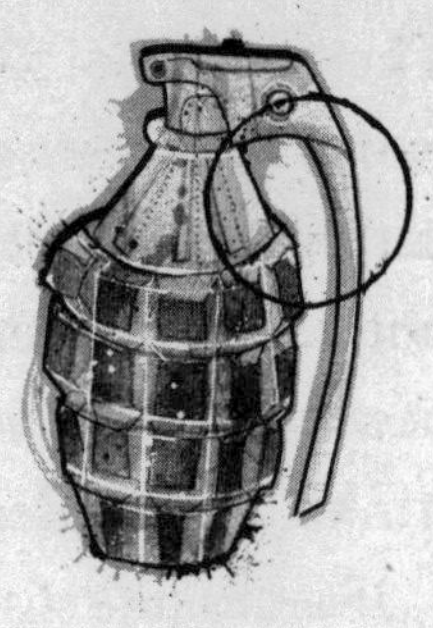

'No,' said Mattie. 'But dogs are.'

'You're right!' gasped her mother. 'Now that you mention it, I remember that the Queen was followed out of your bedroom by six corgis, and the last one looked decidedly shifty.'

'I saw it too,' said Mattie, 'in the hall as they were leaving. I remember thinking, that's a strange-looking corgi. It looks more like a mole! Gosh, I think we've cracked it. I bet that's our thief; the strange looking corgi at the back!'

'Not so fast,' cautioned her mother. 'We can't just go around accusing the Queen's corgis without proof. She could have us clapped in irons for the rest of our lives.'

'Then we'll just have to *get* proof,' said Mattie. 'We'll just have to search the Queen's Palace until we find that key-ring.' But getting in to search a queen's palace is not as easy as it sounds.

Meanwhile, two revenge-crazed moles were sitting opposite each other in the witch doctor's surgery.

The witch doctor mole was writing on a piece of ivory-coloured card with a quill pen. He curled the last 'h' of Elizabeth, then sat back and pushed the finished document across the table to Old Three-Paws.

'All done,' he said. 'One forged invitation inviting Mattie to the Queen's forthcoming garden party. Careful not to smudge the ink!'

The three-pawed mole was deeply impressed. 'Is there anything you can't do?' he asked.

The witch doctor pointed to the silver box in the corner of his room. 'I'm not very good at setting the video,' he said.

***

At three o'clock the following morning, a very short postman with a pronounced limp delivered a letter to Mattie's house. When Mattie opened her royal invitation she could not believe her good fortune.

'Sometimes, I think I've got a fairy godmother,' said the murderer of moles. 'I mean, how lucky am I? One day I really want to get into the Queen's palace to conduct a search for Moley but I don't know how, and the next I get an invitation to a royal garden party!'

HRH The Queen Invites YOU

Mattie Bleurgh

2

A Royal Garden Party

At

The Palace

When? Next Week!

Bring a bottle

Mattie and her mother were dolled up to the nines when they arrived at the palace for the garden party, but Mattie never saw the garden. She snuck inside and spent her time dodging security while she hunted for Moley. She looked everywhere, from dungeon to tower, from banqueting hall to throne room. She checked behind portraits, suits of armour and gun racks. She turned out wine cellars, servants and boxes of old toys. She looked under the corgis,

inside liveried footmen's footwear and behind old Beefeaters from a bygone age. But nowhere did she find it.

Then, just as she was leaving, she happened to glance at the hall table where the Queen's car keys were lying in the Queen's car-key bowl. And there it was. Soft, smooth, silky-grey and bloodstained with happy memories!

* * *

'Excuse me, miss.' The beefeater had crept up behind Mattie while she was slipping Moley into her pocket.

She hadn't noticed he was there. 'Sorry?' she said, suddenly waking up to the danger.

'I believe you've got something there that belongs to Her Majesty.'

'No,' Mattie lied. 'Are you accusing me of theft?'

'A key-ring, perhaps?'

'I don't know what you mean. My daddy was a prime minister.'

'And my daddy was a thief,' said the beefeater, 'which is why I'm so good at catching them.'

Mattie was charged, tried and sent down for three years, to a correctional institution for naughty children. One week into her sentence, she was already bored and complaining that she had nothing to do. After a childhood spent blowing up moles with fireworks, prison life seemed a little tame by comparison. So imagine her delight when one of the warders announced that she had a visitor.

'How unexpected,' said Mattie.

'You can say that again,' said the warden. It was the Queen.

***

Helpful Hints On How To Deal With Gruesome Grown-ups

3. THE QUEEN

In 'Silence Is Golden', you found out that you can tell what a lady is like from the contents of her handbag. But this does not apply to the Queen. Do NOT look in the Queen's handbag to see what sort of lady she is or you will find out quicker than you think. She will have you arrested by a small army, hung, drawn and quartered on live TV, and fed to the ravens in the Tower of London. OK?

They sat on Mattie's bed and talked like old friends.

'One used to strangle moles oneself, you know,' confessed the Queen. 'when one was a princess. So one is familiar with the lovely smell and feel of moleskin.'

'I can't live without it, Your Majesty.'

'No. And for that reason one is granting you—'

Mattie jumped up excitedly. 'Not a pardon!' she shrieked.

'No. Not a pardon—' Mattie sat down again '—another chance,' said the Queen.

'Oh,' mumbled Mattie, as the Queen reached into her handbag and took something out.

'One wants you to have this,' she said, pressing a small, warm object into Mattie's hand.

'It's Moley!' she cried.

'Yes,' said the Queen, 'and you can keep it!'

'Are you sure?' gasped the prisoner.

'Well, it was yours to begin with, dear . . . and don't look so surprised that one should know. One extracted a confession from the corgis. Apparently a rather brazen mole infiltrated their number without them knowing and left it on my pillow.' She stood up and walked towards the door. 'So, is one happy?' she asked, even though she already knew the

answer. She had only to look at Mattie's beatific smile, as she sniffed the fur and rubbed the silky soft paw across her cheek, to realise that the next three years were going to fly past for this happy girl.

What the Queen was not telling Mattie, however, was that she no longer wanted to keep Moley. Every morning since the accursed thing had been in her possession, strange things had been occurring to the royal face! Things that could be traced back directly to the curse of a certain three-legged mole!

* * *

Old Three-Paws switched on the witch doctor's video recorder and slipped in a tape.

'You mean a curse can sometimes overspill and affect others?' he said, selecting the Sports Channel.

'Only if they're guilty of the same offence,' said the witch doctor, settling into his favourite armchair and dragging it round to face the telly.

'There.' The three-pawed mole handed the remote control to its owner. 'That's got it working.'

'Excellent. I can record the cricket now.' Then the witch doctor mole pressed RECORD with his four fat fingers and hit FAST FORWARD instead.

***

For three years, Mattie lay happily in her prison cell snuggled up to Moley. For three years, the soft grey fur never left the skin on her face. For three long years she was blissfully unaware of The Curse of the Old Three-Paws. Then, come the day of her release, she was told to smarten up her appearance before stepping outside and, for the first time since she had been locked up, she was given a mirror.

It was a cruel way to find out. As Mattie raised the mirror to her face she did not recognise herself. Her face was covered in mole-coloured fur! She screamed and dropped the mirror, but as it hit the floor the angle of the glass revealed an even worse truth. It was not just her face that was furry; the curse of Old Three-Paws had covered her whole body in moleskin from the top of her head to the tips of her velvety toes!

'I'm a mole!' she cried. 'Dig-diggerdy-do!'

But that was not all. When Mattie the mole maimer went home she was so ashamed of the way

she looked that she refused to let her mother see her. She ran into her bedroom, ripped up her floorboards, jumped into the hole and started digging to get as far away as she possibly could from the light.

Little did she know where she was heading. Suffice to say that the final part of the curse condemned her to live underground for ever in The Darkness!

THE CURSE OF OLD THREE-PAWS

I CURSE YOU, MATTIE BLEURGH, TO LOSE NOT ONLY YOUR PRECIOUS FATHER (PART 1) BUT YOUR PRECIOUS MOLEY TOO (PART 2) AND TO BE SO ANXIOUS TO GET IT BACK THAT YOU WILL COMMIT A CRIME FOR WHICH YOU WILL BE BANGED UP LONG-TERM. THIS MEANS THAT FOR THREE YEARS YOU WILL ONLY HAVE MY SEVERED PAW FOR COMPANY (PART 3). THREE YEARS OF CONTACT WITH MY DEAD FUR *AND* NO MIRRORS! THAT SHOULD DO IT. AND WHEN IT'S DONE, IT'S THE DARKNESS FOR YOU (PART 4).

She arrived at Main Reception after sixteen days of non-stop digging, and now lives in a network of tunnels that I'd specially prepared for her under Rooms 101, 102, 103, 104, 105, 106, 107, 108 and 109. When YOU come to stay maybe you can play with her. You'd enjoy a game of Hunt the Mole, and I'll provide the giant rockets!

By the way, if ever you should ever happen to be lurking outside the Queen's bathroom and hear electric shaving from within, accompanied by an old lady's voice cursing her whiskers thus;

'Be gone foul moleskin!'

Now you'll know why!

Next time you look at a stamp or a five pound note see if you can spot the difference.

Now, take a look at this photograph.

As you can see, it is the photograph of a girl and her parents. Nothing unusual in that, except that where else would you find a daughter who was older than her parents? The photograph was taken in 1965 when the parents were six years old and best friends at primary school. The daughter was snapped thirty years later when she was eleven. And here's another strange thing: the parents are smiling whereas the girl is not. But I don't want you feeling sorry for the girl. Punishments are never handed out without just cause and in this girl's case there was cause aplenty!

THE SOUL STEALER

Poppy was a vicious gossip-monger who owned not one, but *six* mobile phones so that she could conduct simultaneous six-way conversations with her six brainless best friends. They would blather from morning till night. From the moment her pretty empty little head woke up, through breakfast, break and lunch, and for the whole six hours between school ending and bedtime starting, Poppy's mouth spouted rumours and lies till her lips were numb!

So greatly did her parents hate this mindless chatter that they came up with a cruel but cunning scare tactic to wean their daughter off her phones. It was breakfast time one morning, and Poppy had just spent forty-eight minutes discussing the colour of her socks with Millie, Molly, Mickey, Mandy, Dreena and Ash while her bacon got cold.

'You do know what mobile phones *do*, don't you?' said her father, the second after she'd hung up. 'Recent scientific research has proved that mobile phones microwave brains!'

Poppy's mother gasped theatrically. 'Imagine what must be happening inside your head, Poppy! Think of all that damage you're doing to your brain by using *six* phones all the time!'

'I wouldn't be surprised,' continued her father, laying on the horror with a trowel, 'if your brains hadn't been microwaved into scrambled egg by now!'

'Not poached, not boiled, but *scrambled*!' echoed her mother. 'Next time you put your head on one side your brain'll dribble out your ear!'

Poppy had a nightmare vision of sitting in a cinema and putting her head on her boyfriend's shoulder (prior to a smooch), only to find that scrambled egg was pouring out of her ear and dripping down his shirt!

'I know what you're doing,' she scoffed. 'You're trying to stop me gossiping by splitting me up from my phones. Well, here's some fresh gossip. You've *failed*! I'm not getting rid of them.'

'Not even if we were to replace all six with a

Nokisson 5000?' Poppy's father was fiendishly clever. The Nokisson 5000 had a digital camera. It was the all-singing, all-dancing, must-have mobile that every child wanted!

Twenty-four hours later, Poppy had swapped six mobiles for one. Instead of improving her behaviour, however, the N5000 simply made it worse. It was no longer the witless chattering that caused the problem, it was the camera. The camera made Poppy smug and conceited, because amongst her circle of school friends it made her the centre of attention. Everyone wanted their picture taken. In the playground, girlfriends clamoured around her and fought each other for a glimpse of the lens.

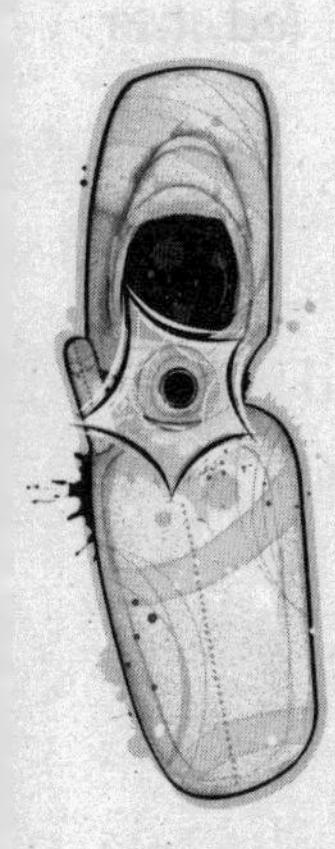

'Me, Poppy. Me!' they screamed.

'Ow!'

'Get off my pigtails!'

'Over here!'

'CHEESY CHEESE! My smile's the biggest!' You'd have thought none of them had ever seen a camera before!

They'll see a camera when they get down here that's for sure. It's the one I use to take mug shots of all of my guests. It's called a Single Reflex Griffin. It's got the head of an eagle and the body of a lion, so when I tell my photographic subjects to 'Watch the birdie!' what I really mean is; 'Watch OUT for the birdie, because it hates children who wriggle and will rip out your throat if you don't sit still!' That's why it's called a Single Reflex, because that's the only reflex it knows.

One girl *hated* the camera. She was new to the school and her name was Ana. She had lost both parents in a holiday accident whilst photographing them in front of a cable car. One minute they were there, the next they had gone. The police enquiry concluded that they had slipped over the cliff, but Ana thought she knew differently.

She was responsible. Why else had she been sent to live with Mr Chan, an uncle who she hardly knew? A strange old man who kept his mouth shut and his head lowered, as if his eyes were deadly weapons, a man who rarely spoke except to fill her head with stories about the Soul Stealer . . .

Mr Chan ran the local supermarket around the corner from the school, where the bad girls used to hang out and steal stuff.

'It's easy,' they said, when they initiated younger girls into their gang. 'You can nick anything and he never sees you, because he hasn't got CCTV. He's scared of cameras. Thinks all those pictures are full of demons!'

***

When Poppy chased Ana with her N5000 camera phone, Ana froze with fear.

'Don't point that thief at me!' she shouted. 'Go away!'

'Thief?' Poppy sniggered. '*Thief!* Which century were you born in?' Then to the amusement of her cronies, Poppy articulated each word individually as if Ana couldn't understand. 'A *THIEF* STEALS CANDLESTICKS AND WALLETS. THIS IS A PHONE, ANA. UNDERSTAND? IT HAS A CAMERA INSIDE IT. YOU KNOW, *FLASH BANG WALLOP*. YOU *DO* KNOW WHAT A CAMERA IS, DON'T YOU?'

'Take that thief away!' Ana wailed.

'But I haven't stolen anything,' jeered Poppy.

'You don't know what Mr Chan has told me,' replied Ana. 'You will steal my soul.'

'Let's see, shall we?' said Poppy, pressing the button that clicked the shutter and flashed the flash in her eyeballs. Ana screamed and ran away. 'Don't you want your soul back?' Poppy mocked, holding her camera aloft like a trophy. The other girls crowded around in a froth of hysteria.

'Oh, Poppy!' they screeched. 'You are *so* funny!'

Carried away on this wave of adoration Poppy dismissed Ana as a screwball and used the camera to instigate a reign of terror in the playground. By starting a brand new sport that nobody else could play – Poppy's Photo Blackmail – she unleashed the bad girl inside of her!

Did you know that there's bad inside everybody? They don't tell you, but it lives inside the appendix. That's why so many people have them cut out. And do you know where all those appendixes go? They give them to me. I store them in my freezer and when I want children to be even badder than they already are, I give them one to suck, like a lolly!

The first time Poppy played the blackmail game was in the school loos. She shoved her camera under the cubicle door and snapped a prefect on the pan.

'Oy! What's going on?' cried the victim.

'You have just been captured on my camera,' said Poppy, 'and unless you give me all the sweets in your pocket I shall put this photo on the noticeboard.'

'But everyone will see it,' cried the girl with no pants.

'Oh yes,' sniggered Poppy. 'I hadn't thought of that.' A crumpled paper bag full of sweets shot out under the door into Poppy's grasp. 'I hope you washed your hands!' she roared. 'Ha ha!'

During lunch, she hid behind the bike sheds and leaped out on a pair of secret lovers, interrupting their illicit kissing with a flash of her Nokisson.

'Oy! You two! That snog's going to cost you dear.'

The boy burst into tears when Poppy demanded his cap in return for not showing the photos to the head teacher. 'Please, Poppy,' he wailed. 'Don't tell anyone. I'm going out with Donna and if she finds

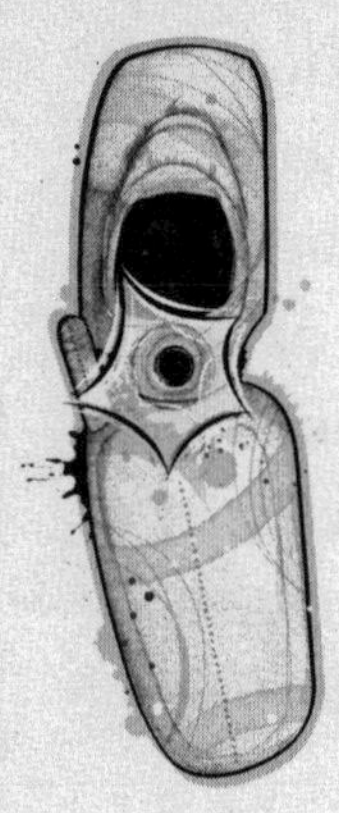

out I've been kissing another girl, she'll kill me.'

'That *is* Donna,' said Poppy.

'Is it?' said the boy, turning to the girl he'd just pulled. 'Are you Donna?'

'Yes,' she said. The boy looked confused.

'Who am I going out with then?'

Poppy hung around the bus stop and caught her classmates copying homework off each other. She hooked her feet over the edge of the shelter roof, dropped down in front of them like a spider, and took an upside-down photograph of their cheating to hold them to account.

'Teacher's going to see what I've just seen,' she smirked. 'You are in such trouble.'

'You can't!' said the girl, whose homework the boy was copying.

'You wouldn't!' said the boy who hadn't been listening in class.

'I would and I could . . . but I won't,' said Poppy. 'Not if you do my homework for a year!'

The boy gasped. 'A year!'

'All right . . . two!' said Poppy. 'Say Hard Cheese!'

And she took a second photo just to rub it in.

***

Over the next few weeks, Poppy used her camera to humiliate as many of her school friends as she could. It was a power trip. She loved the fact that she could control other people's lives and nobody could stop her. She loved it so much, in fact, that she extended her blackmailing to grown-ups.

This was her mistake. Some grown ups CAN be blackmailed; some CAN'T! Get it wrong at your peril!

Poppy blackmailed her mother first. She was in a field picking primroses when Poppy popped up from behind a tussock and digitally captured her on her phone.

'It's hardly a criminal offence,' her mother protested.

'I think you'll find that the Wildlife and Countryside Act of 1981 expressly forbids the picking of wild flowers. *You* might not think it's important, but there are several policemen who will.'

Her mother realised that she had been caught red-handed. 'What do you want this time?' she sighed.

'Full control over the TV remote on Tuesdays, Thursdays and Saturdays.'

For once Poppy's demands were not unreasonable. 'Fine,' said her mother, thinking she had got off lightly.

'And a holiday in Ibiza,' added Poppy slyly. 'Smile for the camera!'

Dippy mothers can be blackmailed.

Poppy caught her grandmother sneaking out of the Betting Shop having had a naughty flutter on *Lucky Pensioner* in the 3.30 at Rhyl.

'Poppy!' shrieked her granny, as the photograph was taken. 'You little sneak!'

'I'll take those winnings, Granny, unless you want me to report you to Gamblers Anonymous!' Then with no respect for age, she relieved her granny of ninety five pounds and ran off down the road to buy an iPod.

Lying grandmothers can be blackmailed.

Her fat father was a target too. He had been on a diet for as long as Poppy could

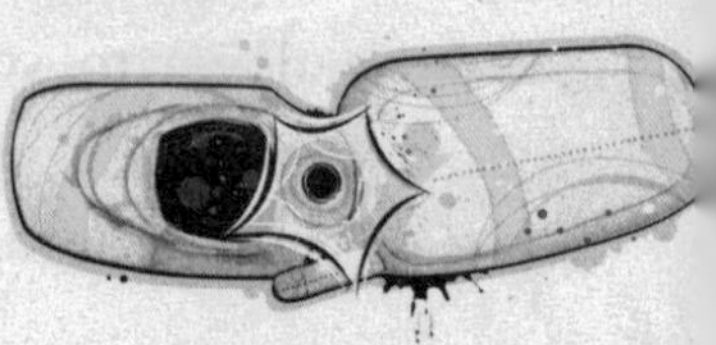

remember, yet despite her mother's best efforts he had never lost a pound. Her mother was baffled, but Poppy knew why. Every night her father would sneak downstairs and raid the fridge. All she had to do was wait and catch him with his snout in the trough!

Click. Poppy switched on her spotlight and lit up the fridge. Trapped in the shaft of light, Poppy's guilty father froze. In one hand he held a beer. in the other a pork pie and wedged between his teeth a chocolate orange.

'That snack's going to cost you big time, diet boy!' she said as she snapped his photo.

'It wasn't me!' he lied pathetically.

But Poppy stood her ground. 'The camera never lies, Dad. Mum will only see the truth.'

'OK,' he blubbed, scoffing the pork pie to comfort himself. 'What do you want this time?'

'I shall be filling that in with many excellent excuses,' she said, handing him a sheaf of letters. 'All you have to do is sign it.'

He read the one on top. '*Poppy cannot come to school today because* . . . Where's the rest of it?'

'That's down to you,' she said. 'You have to make up an excuse and then sign it. Aren't you proud of your little daughter, Daddy? There's one

letter for every day of the school year!' If you can believe it, her father did as he was told and all for fear of his wife finding out that he was a midnight porker!

Feeble fathers can be blackmailed.

In case you hadn't gathered yet, Poppy's prying eye had turned her into a bully. But bullies always come a cropper. They never think they will but they always do.

They make the best guests too, because they are such big cowards. Tough in front of their friends, but put them in the Presidential Suite of Pain and they're all screams and pleadings to go home to mummy!

WHAT DID YOU SAY? SPEAK UP. I CAN'T HEAR YOU.

I said, it's semolina tonight, Jumbo. Your favourite.

***

The next day, Poppy spotted Ana in the street and ran across the road to block the younger girl's path.

'Hello, Ana,' she grinned as she slid the camera phone out of her pocket. 'I've come to steal your soul!'

Ana yelped and took off like a small Jack Russell. She slid through Poppy's legs, ran round the corner and dashed across the zebra-crossing into Mr Chan's supermarket. When Poppy caught up, Ana was hiding behind Mr Chan's legs. Poppy laughed contemptuously. He was not a tall man. In fact, he had a pigeon chest and a thin bony face. Not the sort of grown up to cause Poppy any trouble.

Or so she thought! Thin old shopkeepers called Mr Chan CAN'T be blackmailed!

'What do you want?' he said calmly, keeping his eyes fixed on the floor. 'No cameras allowed in here. Take that camera outside!' He pointed to the door.

'Why?' sneered Poppy. 'It's only a little snap.'

'If Ana says she does not want her picture taken, you must respect this.'

'You still haven't told me why,' jeered Poppy.

'Because she believes that the camera can kill a person by stealing their soul.'

'You've taught her this, have you?' said Poppy. 'It's a load of old rubbish!'

'Be careful what you say.' Mr Chan took hold of Poppy's arm and dragged her to one side. 'Ana's parents are dead,' he whispered. 'They died in an accident, slipping over a cliff, but she believes that they live on in her photographs. Ana is still little. She believes what she needs to believe to make her happy.'

'Well she needs to grow up,' sneered Poppy, 'because taking someone's photograph doesn't kill them.'

'It does if you take *this* man's photograph.' Mr Chan produced a battered photo from his pocket. It was a sepia print of an old Chinaman with wrinkled skin, long grey hair and a thin, bootlace moustache. 'He is powerful spirit what need to be fed. This is the Soul Stealer!'

'He looks so *un*scary!' shrieked Poppy. 'In fact he looks like you. Is it you?' She prodded Mr Chan in the shoulder.

'No!' shouted Ana all of a sudden. 'Don't do that.'

The old man did not flinch, but replied in a voice as cold as ice. 'If I am, know this. No one who takes a photograph of the Soul Stealer ever lives to take another. Now go, before it is too late.'

But Poppy was intrigued. 'I want to know what you're going to do to me if I take your

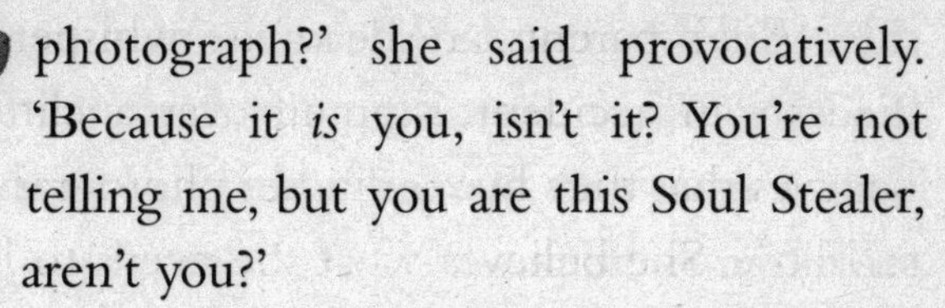

photograph?' she said provocatively. 'Because it *is* you, isn't it? You're not telling me, but you are this Soul Stealer, aren't you?'

'He will take the life part of you and lock it into a picture for ever.'

'Oh yeah?' sniffed Poppy. 'So tell me this, oh wise uncle of the big cry-baby, how come the old bearded Chinaman who hates having his photo taken so much is in that photograph in your hand?'

'Because,' said Mr Chan in a calmly measured voice that sent a shiver down Poppy's spine, 'the man who took this photograph is now dead.'

Poppy laughed nervously. 'You mean the Soul Stealer, or should I say *you*, killed him just because you didn't like the picture?'

'Do not mock the Soul Stealer,' he warned, 'or he will steal your soul away. I suggest you leave now while you can still save your worthless bones!'

'You actually *believe* all this mumbo jumbo, don't you!' scoffed Poppy, raising the camera to her eye.

'Because it's TRUE!' screamed Ana, but her intervention came too late. Mr Chan looked up as Poppy pressed the button on her camera phone. As

the flashlight exploded she saw something flicker in his eyes. They were camera shutters: diamond-shaped irises that opened and closed in the time it took him to blink.

***

Later that night, Poppy printed out her photographs. She was admiring her gallery of shame, as villains are wont to do, when she noticed something that made her blood run cold. In the photograph she had taken in the supermarket, Mr Chan's face had changed. The skin had wrinkled, the hair had grown long and grey and on the top lip sat a thin, bootlace moustache. It was the face of the Soul Stealer.

She looked through her other photographs and was horrified to see the same face staring back at her from the corner of each one. And alongside this face mysterious objects started to appear – dismembered body parts like the building bricks of a corpse. First a hand; then a hand and a foot; then a hand, a foot and a knee; then legs, arms and a torso. Suddenly there was the same headless figure in the bottom corner of each and every

photograph. Even without a head she recognised it. It was *her.*

Now Poppy was nervous.

'What am I doing in my own photographs?' she trembled, jabbing her finger at the Soul Stealer. 'This is you, isn't it? This is your doing!'

The bootlace moustache twitched as the image stirred. 'I have stolen your soul!' it declared in a voice that roared, and sounded not unlike the voice of Mr Chan.

In horror, Poppy watched as *her* head materialised on top of the headless figures. In the picture, she had a digital camera pressed to her eye and her mouth was moving. 'Watch the birdie, me!' said her photographic self. There was a flash as Poppy took her own photograph. Then she was gone, leaving the room cold and empty.

Ana never saw Poppy again. Poppy's parents never saw Poppy again either. Not in the flesh. A few days later, her mother found a copy of the black and white photograph behind the fridge.

'How did this get here?' she exclaimed. 'I haven't

seen this photograph for years. Look, George!' Poppy's father raised his head from his su-doku puzzle.

'Is that the photograph of us at primary school together?' he asked.

'Yes,' said Poppy's mother. As she peered more closely at the image, her voice suddenly trembled and faltered. 'I don't remember Poppy being there, do you?'

'She wasn't born,' he said. Which, of course, she wasn't.

Yet there she was in full-blown colour. Poppy's stolen soul had been torn from the living world and sent to live in that black and white photograph for ever. And *that*, in case you hadn't worked it out for yourself, is why she's always crying!

Of course I should point out that the photograph the parents have is only a copy. The REAL photograph in which the real Poppy is imprisoned lives down here in The Darkness . . . in a shoebox. in the spidery attic where creeping damp and mould can slowly do its worst on the paper. By my reckoning Poppy has another ninety-three years to live before she is entirely consumed by mildew!

Aaaaaaaaaaaagh! This is a nightmare!

Welcome to the Darkness, Nobby

I've saved the MOST GRUESOME GROWN-UPS till last. It's not that they're evil, it's just that they're a GRUESOME SIGHT! This is because there is rather a lot of unnecessary nudity in this story. Because of this adult content I'm afraid I must ask you to sign the disclaimer below, just to cover me in the event of your parents catching you reading the story and wanting to take me to court. There's NO NEED TO READ the disclaimer, it's all PERFECTLY ABOVE BOARD. JUST SIGN IT and let's get on. It's nothing more than a completely HARMLESS STATEMENT saying that it's not my fault if you find the story a bit too rude and die of shock. Honest.

Thank you very much!

DISCLAIMER

I WON'T CAUSE TROUBLE!

If you use this disclaimer as a donor card and my signature as proof that I donate my body and all its contents be it whole or in several little bits to the Hothell Darkness.

SIGNED: *(In blood, please)*

....

The worst thing about dreams is that sometimes you can't tell where the dreaming stops and real life begins. You're lying in the bath when a red-hot buzz saw drops through the ceiling and spins towards your skull. Is it real or are you dreaming? Should you move out of its way or let it slice through your brain? And if you let it chop your brain into slivers of salami will you live to regret it when you get the call to appear on Mastermind? Is your father a spaceman? Does your mother have a tail? And are those real vampire teeth in your teacher's mouth or plastic ones? When you can't tell the difference, life becomes just that little bit more problematic.

NOBBY'S NIGHTMARE

Nobby's problems began when he was walking out with the girl of his dreams. After much discussion, they had decided not to feed the ducks and go to the cinema instead. Their hearts were pounding as they strolled through the busy pedestrian precinct holding hands in a rather self-conscious way. They wanted everyone to think that they held hands all the time, which would make today no big deal, but that was a lie. This was a first and both their hands were sweaty.

'All right, Sophie?' he said.

'All right, Nobby!' she replied, removing the chewing gum from her mouth and sticking it to the trunk of a tree.

'Having a good time?'

'Luvly!' She unwrapped another piece of chewing gum and popped it in her mouth. Then she screwed up the paper and dropped it on the

ground. 'Here,' she said casually. 'I haven't lost my clothes too, have I?'

'What?' Nobby's heart stopped as he looked down and saw pink. 'Oh nuts! I'm naked!' But that was not all. Out of the corner of his eye he realised that Sophie had changed too. She was green and knobbly. 'Aaagh!' he screamed. 'And you've turned into an alien.'

'Of course I have,' she said, hitching her wide, flat bottom over her knees so that she could walk. 'An alien's the only thing in the universe that would walk out with a rudey-nudey like you.'

'But I can't go out with someone who's green,' panicked Nobby, horribly aware of the warts and calluses that had suddenly appeared on Sophie's hand.

'You liked me a minute ago,' she said, clinging on to his fingers as he tried to disentangle them from hers.

'People will laugh!' he cried, as passers-by stopped and stared.

'Oh dear. Well if you can't see beyond my skin colour,' she said, turning to face him. 'I'm afraid I'm going to have to eat you.'

'What? NO!' Nobby's heart pounded in his ears while inside his head a loud voice yelled

'Wake up! Wake up!' As Sophie drew back her lips and flashed a row of fearsomely sharp teeth, Nobby pinched himself all over. 'I can't feel a thing!' he wailed. 'This must be real.'

'Sorry!' smiled Sophie, lunging towards him like a giant grain-pecking chicken on steroids.

Nobby put his arms in front of his face to fend her off. 'NO!' he screamed. 'NO!' But her blunt beak was too powerful. 'Aaaaaagh!'

And then he woke up.

'Wuh!' He sat up in bed with sweat beading his top lip. Sophie really *was* the girl of his dreams.

His bad ones!

Whenever he dreamed about her, which was all the time, he always ended up naked. He'd been to see dream doctors about what these dreams meant, but they'd all offered the same interpretation . . . that Nobby clearly *wanted* to be naked with Sophie and his dream was a manifestation of that. But Nobby knew this to be bunkum. He knew the real reason why he always ended up in the buff. It was his parents. They were to blame. They were to blame for everything!

* * *

Just then, the bedroom door opened and Nobby's parents walked in. His dad was carrying a comic that he'd just ironed and his mother was carrying a tray full of food. Both of them were naked – their bits were hanging out for the entire world to see.

'Morning, Nobby,' said his father, opening the curtains with a flourish.

'Brought your breakfast,' said his mother, placing the tray on top of Nobby's legs. 'Two boiled eggs today.'

'And a buttered soldier,' added his father, laying the comic on the duvet.

Nobby's parents were naturists.

* * *

For as long as Nobby could remember, his parents had embarrassed him with their hairy hobby. They had joined a naturist club when he was still in his pram. In those days they took him with them, but when he stopped needing a nappy he refused to go. It curled his toes to sit in the games room and watch his parents playing ping-pong and rummicub in the raw. In fact, as far as Nobby was concerned, *everything* at that naturist club was unnatural. They had a cinema where they watched films in the nude, they had shops where they shopped in the nude and they had barbecues where they cooked in the nude. And when there was a fancy-dress party they did that in the nude as well. Only everyone went as the same two people.

Helpful Hints on How To Deal With Gruesome Grown-Ups

4. IF YOUR PARENTS ARE NATURISTS . . .

Break the tumble dryer and buy an industrial mangle. Then while your father is turning the handle and your mother is feeding your clothes through the rollers, fire a pebble at their bare cheeks with a catapult. They will leap forward and catch their bits in the mangle, and with bits as mangled as that they will never want to show them in public again!

'No don't tell me. Let me guess who you've come as. Is it Adam and Eve?'

What made Nobby's life even worse, however,

was that his parents didn't wear clothes at home, either. Nobby was fed up with sharing the sofa with his parents' rolls of fat, and there was something not entirely savoury about eating a pork pie with your father's bellybutton winking at you over the top of the table.

'There's nothing wrong with taking your clothes off in the privacy of your own home,' his mother said repeatedly. 'Everyone's the same underneath, Nobby.'

'Not true,' he said, checking out her dimpled bottom. 'Some of us are a bit lumpier.'

* * *

Thanks to Nobby's awful parents Nobby's life was a nightmare. He had no friends, because every time one of his schoolmates came round to ask Nobby out, they had to run the gruesome gauntlet of wobbly pink bits. It didn't matter whether the bits were wobbling behind the vacuum cleaner or swinging behind the lawn mower, it was still a horrible sight, and once they'd copped an eyeful Nobby's friends never came back. Little wonder then that Nobby longed to be rid of his parents. With them gone, his life would be normal and he could finally ask Sophie round.

***

Then one day, Nobby's living nightmare took an unexpected twist. He came down for breakfast to find his parents standing in the hall with their clothes *on*.

'We're going out,' said his mother. 'We're taking a bus to the naturist club.' Thankfully, that was one thing his parents never did. Hit the streets naked.

'It's an afternoon of Nude Olympics!' explained his father. 'Why don't you come?'

'Oh go on,' said his mother. 'It's going to be such fun.'

But there was not a bone in Nobby's body that shared her enthusiasm. 'I'm busy,' he sneered. 'Wearing clothes and being normal.'

'You'll be here all on your own if you don't come,' she added, thinking that being on his own would put Nobby off. It hadn't crossed her mind that it might appeal to him. And it did, because this was the opportunity that Nobby had been waiting for. This was the chance to put his master plan into operation.

***

He secretly followed them to the naturist club, waited until they were inside, had stripped off and were playing badminton with a bearded couple called the Hendersons, then sneaked in and stole every piece of clothing on site. With nothing of their own, or anyone else's to wear, Nobby's parents were now trapped inside the club for ever. They couldn't get home unless they walked down the street or went on a bus in the nude, and even *they* weren't prepared to do that! His plan had worked. His life was finally free from embarrassment. Nobby's nightmare was over!

Now that he could do what he liked, he phoned up Sophie and said in his sexiest voice, 'All right, Sophie?'

'All right, Nobby!' she replied.

'Having a good time?' he said.

'Luvly!'

'Doing anything tonight?'

'Washing my hair.'

'Fancy going out?'

'With you?'

'Yeah.'

'Sure,' she said. And Nobby, not unreasonably, thought that *that* was that.

What Nobby didn't know was that nightmares are never over! Like Great White Sharks they just dive under the surface for a bit then come back up when you're least expecting it and bite your head off! That's the beauty of nightmares; they never stop and you never know when you're in one!

Nobby was just putting the phone down when he heard Sophie still talking on the other end of the line. He lifted the receiver back to his ear. 'Sorry,' he said. 'What did you say?'

'I said I'll bring my parents round to meet your parents tonight then.'

'What?' he gasped. 'You want *your* parents to meet *my* parents?'

'I can't go out with you if they don't like you and your family!' she said.

But he didn't *have* any parents. He'd just got rid of them. This was unbelievable timing. Seconds away from pulling the girl of his dreams and suddenly she wants to meet his parents who weren't there! This couldn't be happening to him. He clutched at his chest where a stabbing pain was tearing through his ribs. Oh great! Now he was having a heart attack!

And that was when he woke up.

'Wuh!' He was in the sitting room in an armchair. 'Yes!' he cried with relief. 'I was dreaming! She doesn't want her parents to meet mine after all! Yes! It was just a bad dream! YES!'

But then he looked around the room and saw his parents sitting on the sofa opposite him. They would have been naked had it not been for the saucepans that were strategically placed over their rude bits.

'NO!' howled Nobby. 'What are *you* doing here?

'You came and fetched us,' said his mother. 'Most inconvenient timing it was too.'

'No, I didn't!' protested Nobby. 'That was in my dream.' His eyes lit up suddenly. 'That's it!' he yelled. 'I'm dreaming this as well, aren't I? Please,' he begged. 'Tell me you're just figments of my imagination.'

'You said there was an emergency,' she continued. 'You told us to drop our shuttlecocks and come right away.'

'Only some joker had nicked our clothes,' said Nobby's father. 'So you gave us these saucepans and brought us home on the bus.'

'You told us we had to meet

your girlfriend's parents,' said his mother.

Nobby pinched himself hard. 'You mean this is really happening?' he said. 'Then why can't I feel anything?' He frantically punched the top of his arm as the doorbell rang.

'That'll be them!' he squeaked. 'They're here.'

'Aren't you going to answer it?' asked his mother, straightening the magazines on the coffee table.

'No,' snapped Nobby. Then, 'Yes. No. OK! But whatever happens, be normal and keep those saucepans on!'

'We're not ashamed of our bodies,' said his father.

'No,' said Nobby, 'but I am.'

***

In the hall, Nobby checked his face in the mirror hoping to find proof that he was still in the middle of a nightmare. Did he have horns, for example, or a forked tongue or pixie ears? Sadly, everything was normal. That meant Sophie really *was* outside with her parents, and *had* been for several minutes. He took a deep breath and opened the front door.

'Hello, everyone,' he said breezily, trying to act

as naturally as he could.

'Where've you been?' snapped Sophie. 'We've been standing out here for ages.'

'So sorry,' cringed Nobby, smiling at the unsmiling adults standing behind his would-be girlfriend. 'Mum and dad were cooking – and, you know how these things happn – they just fell into some saucepans.'

'Nobby!' said Sophie curtly. The tone of her voice told him that he was talking too much. 'These are my parents. Lord and Lady Pinkerton.'

'Lord and Lady . . . Oh . . .' Nobby had no idea they were titled! Now that he looked at them – *his* tweed suit and monocle; *her* blue cardigan and pearls – he could see quite clearly that they were nobs.

'I do hope you're a straight kind of family,' barked Lord Pinkerton in his no nonsense, let's-have-less-of-this-shilly-shallying voice.

'Weirdos won't do for our Soph,' added his wife with gusto.

'No,' blushed Nobby. 'Absolutely not.' All he could think about was his excruciating parents sitting in the other room wearing nothing but saucepans. 'Umm . . . Do come in.'

***

When they walked into the sitting room, Nobby's parents were sitting down.

'Lord and Lady Pinkerton,' gulped Nobby, 'these are my parents.'

Unfortunately for Nobby, his parents had old-fashioned manners. When Lord Pinkerton offered his hand, Nobby's parents stood up and offered theirs.

'Delighted to meet you,' they said as the saucepans clattered to the floor, leaving both-stark-bottom naked!

Nobby screamed and punched his arm again. 'Wake up! Wake up! Wake up!' he yelled, but nothing doing. This was no dream. 'Why are you so embarrassing?' he wailed.

'Who's embarrassed?' said Lady Pinkerton. 'I'm not. My husband's not. Sophie?'

'No,' said the girl of his dreams.

Nobby was gobsmacked. 'You're not embarrassed by my naked parents?' he gasped.

'You should see what my parents look like under their clothes,' laughed Sophie. Up until that moment, Nobby could just about cope, but now . . .

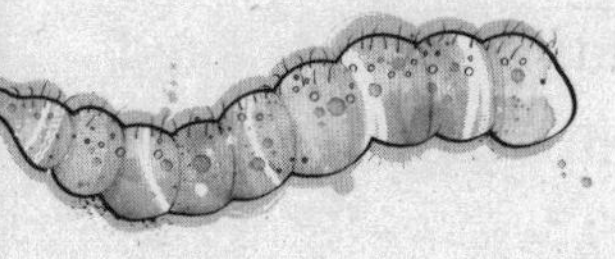

'No. No. No. No. No! They're not going to take their clothes

off as well, are they?' Before he had even finished his sentence he had his answer. 'Oh good gracious, they ARE!' Without any show of surprise from their daughter, Lord and Lady Pinkerton peeled off their clothes and their portly flesh sprang unfettered into the room.

Nobody but Nobby seemed to notice that there were two green aliens with tails, blunt beaks and saggy baggy bellies standing in their sitting room. His naked parents were shaking their guests' flippers and smiling politely.

'We're from the planet Boobletrox,' said the alien formerly known as Lord Pinkerton, 'where naturism is the norm.'

'I can't tell you what a pleasure it is to get those body suits off,' his wife trilled. 'It's the first time since we landed on earth that we don't have to pretend we're somebody we're not. Close your mouth, Nobby dear.'

Nobby's mouth had fallen open with surprise. 'And now that you've met us properly,' announced Sophie's father, 'you have our permission to go out with Sophie.'

Suddenly, Nobby wasn't so sure he wanted to. If the parents were both aliens that made *her* an alien too. Either that or this was another bad dream. He dug his fingernails into the palms of both hands, kicked his own shins and twisted his ear lobes, but nothing woke him up. This was REAL.

'OK,' said Sophie. 'I will go out with Nobby on a trial date, but only on one condition. If *I* have to go naked, so must *he*.'

Now Nobby was really lost. 'What do you mean "go naked"?'

Half an hour later, Nobby's real life was bizarrely imitating his dreams. He and Sophie were strolling through the busy pedestrian precinct holding hands in a rather self-conscious way. He was completely naked, while she had discarded her human form and was waddling along beside him in that menacing way that makes green aliens so scary.

'Stop fidgeting,' she hissed. 'Nobody's looking at *you*. They're all staring at *me*.' Nobby pulled his hand out of her flipper and hid behind a lamppost.

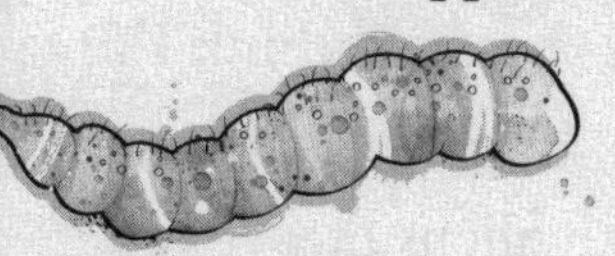

'This is a dream!' he cried. 'Wake up! Wake up! WAKE UP!' But everything he did to

wake himself up just hurt.

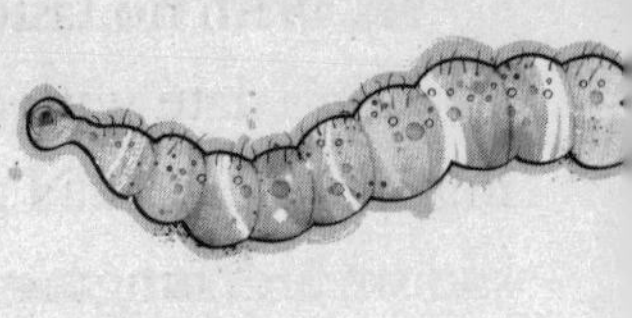

'Of course it hurts,' said Sophie. 'Because all of this is real.'

'It can't be real,' blubbed Nobby. 'This is my worst nightmare. I mean being naked in the street with a hungry alien is . . .' He stopped as a really bad memory resurfaced in his head. 'Oh no! I know what's going to happen next!'

'What?'

'You're going to eat me!'

'Eat you!' Sophie laughed, wetting her beak with the tip of her short black tongue. 'Why would I eat you?' But even as she spoke Nobby knew he was in trouble. Her eyes had suddenly lit up in a way they never had for him. 'Oh look who it is!' she gasped, pointing to a handsome boy who was admiring himself in a shop window on the other side of the street. 'It's Luke Loveaduck. He mustn't see me with you . . .' Nobby was appalled.

'Why not?!' he said. 'I'm your date!'

'In your dreams,' replied Sophie. 'because if he *does* see me with you, he'll think I'm a loser.'

'A loser?'

'Yes. With no taste in men. And he'll never ask me out.' This date with Sophie was turning into a worse nightmare than Nobby's worst nightmare. 'Sorry!' she smiled, lunging towards him like a giant grain-pecking chicken on steroids. Nobby put his arms in front of his face to fend her off.

'NO!' he screamed. 'NO!' But her blunt beak was too powerful. She ate him up with a crunch, a squirt and a bursting eyeball, and as if that wasn't bad enough she then turned back into Sophie and waved at the boy across the street in a rather obvious, I'm-currently-available way!

'Yoo hoo,' she cried. 'Luke! Over here!'

***

And then he woke up!

'Wuh!' Nobby had never been so relieved to discover that everything had just been a terrible dream. His date with Sophie had been so profoundly depressing that he knew it couldn't have been real. Grown-ups *weren't* aliens. Girls *didn't* suddenly turn into green monsters with the appetite to eat a whole boy!

He yawned, but could only open his lips a short way. His mouth was covered in sticky

goo. His eyes were half closed as well, like a newborn baby's. He wasn't quite sure where he was either. He could hear gurgling like an underground stream and distant explosions of gas, like a car backfiring. He rubbed his eyes and cleared away the film.

'Oh!'

Nobby had never been inside an alien's stomach before with its storms of acid rain, its grinding stone walls and its little farty geysers, but since his first nightmare he'd *thought* about it often, and this was exactly what he had imagined it would look like. Which only goes to prove that it was all real and you should never judge a person by the colour of their skin. Some green aliens can be nice, whereas others can eat you. It's just luck, really.

Sweet dreams and don't have nightmares!

Now that you've read everyone's stories is it any clearer why I want you to come and live down here in The Darkness? It's not for me. It's for YOU. Grown-ups are so mean it's NOT SAFE for you up there. If you don't get down here now, how will you know that your mother isn't filling the shampoo bottle with sulphuric acid, or that the milkman isn't lacing your milk with cyanide, or that the new barber doesn't have knives instead of fingers and a no-nonsense way of trimming your head from your shoulders?

You can't know. So don't take the risk.

Come along. It's time to go now. Leave a note for your parents, pack pyjamas and a teddy and let's have no more delay.

OK, let's go. Just lock your bedroom door first so your parents can't barge in and stop us.

I said, 'LOCK THE DOOR!' NOT 'STEP THROUGH IT

COME BACK HERE!
READING SAFETY TIPS
NEVER OPEN THE BOOK AGAIN! HE HAS SEEN YOUR FACE AND HE BEARS GRUDGES